JEWISH

DETECTIVE

STORIES FOR KIDS

First Printing 2001
Second Printing 2004

Published by Pitspopany Press
Copyright © 2001

Cover Design by Ben Gasner Studios
Book Design by Tiffen Studios (T.C. Peterseil)

Pitspopany Press titles may be purchased for fundraising programs by schools and organizations by contacting:

Marketing Director, Pitspopany Press
40 East 78th Street, Suite 16D
New York, New York 10021
Tel: (800) 232-2931
Fax: (212) 472-6253
Email: pop@netvision.net.il

ISBN: 0-930143-14-1   Cloth
ISBN: 0-930143-15-X   Paper

Printed in Israel

To the detective in all of us –

May we follow after the truth, forever.

TABLE OF CONTENTS

JEWISH
DETECTIVE
STORIES FOR KIDS

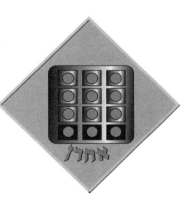

The Mystery Of The Disappearing Dogs

By Dvora Waysman

9

About Dvora Waysman...

Dvora was born in Melbourne, Australia, and came to Israel in 1971 with her husband and four children, now parents themselves of 17 beautiful "sabras".

Dvora lives in Jerusalem and is the author of: *My Long Journey Home, To Any Jewish Teenager: Letters From Jerusalem, Back of Beyond, The Pomegranate Pendant,* and other children's and adult titles.

She was the recipient of the "For Jerusalem" citation for her fiction, poems, and features about the city; and the *Seeff Award* for Best Foreign Correspondent. She is syndicated in 27 newspapers abroad, and has been teaching Creative Writing and Journalism for 28 years.

THE MYSTERY OF
THE DISAPPEARING DOGS

Boring! Boring! Boring! David thought when his grandmother offered him a free overseas holiday if he would travel with her for the summer.

Of course he didn't say it aloud, because he loved her and knew that she was too frail to travel on her own and deal with airports and luggage. But he had really wanted to go to summer camp in the Catskills. He'd had a great time last year. Yet he tried to summon up some enthusiasm for his grandmother's trip.

"Well, where is this place, Jersey?" he asked.

"I've heard it's a very beautiful island, off the coast of England. It's in the Bay of St. Michel, sheltered by the Brittany coast, and it's the largest of the Channel Islands."

"Sounds great!" David lied. "What can you do there?"

His grandmother looked thoughtful. "There are lovely beaches, I believe. And Gerald Durrell's famous zoo. There are lots of farms and a wonderful climate, so my friends tell me. We'll be staying in the main town called St. Helier; it's very French really."

"You mean people talk French there? Like *'La plume de ma tante est sur le table'*" he said, summoning up what he remembered of his ghastly French knowledge.

"Some do," she said smiling, "but they speak English, too."

Trying to maintain an expression of interest while his heart sank, he asked, "Grandma, just why do you want to go to this Jersey?"

"I have friends there that I knew when I was a girl in Poland. Abe and Genia Glickman are like me, Holocaust survivors. We haven't seen each other for sixty years. They settled in Jersey in 1945 when I came to America, just after World War II. Now they've written, inviting me to stay with them for a month."

"Lovely," David enthused. What he was really thinking was, "A month on an island with three geriatrics! What a cool way to spend the summer!" Then he felt ashamed of himself. They had been in concentration camps and undergone shocking experiences and the loss of their families. If he could give his grandmother a little happiness now that Grandpa was gone, by helping her reunite with her friends, of course he must do it and not look at it as a sacrifice. He'd have plenty more summers in his young life.

They traveled by plane to London, and then took a train and a boat the rest of the way.

David had to admit that Jersey was beautiful. In the harbor, the water was a sparkling blue and the marina was full of luxurious yachts that were moored there.

"Must be a lot of rich people in the Channel Islands," he decided.

The Glickmans, however, were not rich. They were a gentle, elderly couple and it was touching to

see their reunion with Sarah Cohen, David's grandmother. They lived with their dog, a spaniel named Rusty, in a charming little cottage with a garden full of sweet-smelling, colorful flowers. They had thought-fully borrowed a bicycle for David so  that he could get around the island, and with Rusty as his companion, David began to enjoy the sunny days.

One day, when he was riding home from the beach, Rusty cavorting at his side, David took a different road. It passed by a farm with a herd of the famous Jersey cows, and a sign that said they sold Royal potatoes, strawberries, and fresh cream. It made his mouth water, and he tried to remember its location so that he could come back one day when he had money and bring back strawberries and cream for Grandma Sarah and the Glickmans.

"Aquila Street," he memorized, "off Rouge Bouillon." The French names were difficult to get his tongue around, but at least his French lessons hadn't been a total loss.

As he was passing a small lane, he saw an overturned bicycle and an old man lying on the road. Hopping off his own bike, he hastened to help him.

"Are you okay?" David asked, taking the man by the elbow and helping him up. "What happened?"

"Stupid! Stupid!" the old man grunted in a guttural accent, "I twist mine ankle and fall off mine bicycle."

"Where do you live?" David asked.

The man pointed to a small cottage just down the road.

"You sit on the seat and I'll wheel you," David offered.

The old man nodded and let David take him home.

"My name's David," David volunteered.

"Carl Heinrich," was the gruff reply.

When David had settled Carl in a chair, he bathed his ankle in cold water and offered to make him a cup of tea, but Mr. Heinrich just waved his hand, dismissing David with a scowl, as though he were a servant. So David left.

"I guess what I did was a 'mitzvah', even though he didn't seem very grateful," he thought.

When he got home, his grandmother and the Glickmans were reading the local paper. "I'm glad you're back," Mrs. Glickman said. "I was worried about Rusty."

"He's fine," David said, puzzled. The dog was lapping up a big bowl of water very thirstily. "He enjoys going to the beach with me."

"It's just these ads in the paper," Grandma Sarah explained. "Every week there are ads from dog owners who have lost their pets. Barely a week goes by that someone's dog doesn't disappear. It's a mystery."

"What do you mean disappearing?"

Mrs. Glickman handed him the paper. There was a big display advertisement and it read:

14

LOST DOG!
German shepherd. Family pet.
Disappeared Wednesday.
Golden, with brown feet.
Answers to the name of Vanilla.
Wears a collar with his name
and telephone number. - **REWARD!**

In the classified ads there were two more under the listing of Lost Dogs. One was a Corgi named Bruno and the other, a Pekingese named Charlie. Both families offered rewards.

"It's been going on for a long time," Mr. Glickman said. "Soon there'll be no dogs left on the island. Rusty is like a child to us," he added. "We couldn't bear to lose him."

"Nothing will happen to Rusty while he's with me," David reassured them.

Over supper David told them about his little adventure with the old man, Carl Heinrich. The Glickmans exchanged glances.

"He's not a very nice man," Mrs. Glickman said. "Don't get too friendly with him."

"Well, he's not exactly the friendly type, or someone I'd choose for a friend."

Mrs. Glickman nodded. "You did a good thing, David. After all, he's a German."

"So what?" David said, a bit annoyed. "I know about the Nazis. But there must be good Germans, too."

"No, you don't understand," Mr. Glickman has-

tened to explain. "During World War II, the Germans overtook and occupied this island. It was the closest they got to England. Lots of German soldiers were sent here, and they ruled over the local people. They were very harsh and it was a nightmare for the people of Jersey.

"For five years, until 1944 when the tide turned for Britain, Germans were the masters here. But when the defeated soldiers left in June of '44, rumor has it that this old man, who wasn't old then of course – I suppose he was in his '20's – hid on the island and stayed here. The Germans couldn't find him to send him back. After a few years they stopped looking and now he lives here openly. He's what you call a recluse, someone who doesn't like people and prefers to be left alone. He must be about 80 by now. He just goes to the shops to buy food now and then. People try to be civil to him, but he never smiles or returns their greetings. You should keep out of his way. Some people think he's crazy."

David nodded. "Sounds right to me. Still, it must be awful not to have any family or friends."

For the next few days, David went off with Rusty to explore other parts of the island, which wasn't very big – only nine miles long by five miles wide.

On his way home from his outings, David would always go past Mr. Heinrich's cottage and knock on the door, offering to go to the shops or chop wood or do whatever he could to help. Mr. Heinrich was still barely able to walk and David could see he was getting low on supplies. Anyway, helping people,

especially elderly people, was something he'd been taught to do all his life by his parents and teachers. You were supposed to help others unselfishly and not expect anything in return. Certainly David wasn't expecting gifts or money. But, while the  old man grudgingly accepted David's offers for help, he never thanked him, or even acknowledged David's presence. All he did was make David feel uncomfortable, mumbling to himself in German.

"He's sort of creepy," David thought. "Probably has dementia or something like that. He really is a crazy person."

When David saw that Mr. Heinrich could manage on his own and his ankle was better, he stopped going there.

One day David decided to go to a part of the island called Fort Regent, a fortress built during the time of Napoleon, which had been converted into a recreation center for the islanders. He made himself some sandwiches and whistled for Rusty. But instead of an excited yap, there was silence. He searched high and low, but there was no sign of the dog. His grandmother and the Glickmans searched, too, and Mrs. Glickman was close to tears. "I knew we would lose him," she cried. "Everyone loses their dog on this island."

"Don't worry, Rusty's probably chasing a cat or something. I'll find him," David reassured her. He set off on his bike and rode everywhere he could think

of...the beach where Rusty had buried a bone...the little streets and alleys near his home where he was taken for walks...even the houses where his dog friends lived.

David remembered that Rusty had once followed a female collie called Susy to her house. The sign on the door said, "The Thompsons" and under it were the names, "James, Helen, Andrew, Sally, and Susy." He knocked on the door. It was opened by a lady around his mother's age.

"I'm sorry to disturb you," David apologized. "My name's David. I'm visiting here with my grandmother. I'm looking for a dog called Rusty. He's a spaniel and belongs to friends of mine. Sometimes he used to sit outside your gate and kind of talk to your dog through the fence. I mean, they both used to bark, but it was almost like they were having a conversation."

Mrs. Thompson sighed, showing him inside. "Susy's gone, too. We can't find her anywhere. My little girl's been crying for days and my son has looked all over the island."

"Where do you think she is?" David asked, suddenly worried that perhaps he really would not find Rusty.

She shrugged. "I came home from shopping on Wednesday, and my front gate was open. I never leave it open. My daughter was at a friend's house. We drove everywhere, but there was no sign of her. She was like a member of the family. If you find your dog, and Susy's with him, I'll give you a reward. Just

18

please return her." The woman was almost crying.

"I don't need a reward. I'll just keep looking for Rusty, and Susy too," he told Mrs. Thompson. David was about to leave, but he could see that his host wanted to talk some more. So, when she offered him a glass of lemonade, he took it and sat down in the kitchen.

"We came to live on Jersey five years ago," she told him, pouring a glass of lemonade for herself as well. "We thought it would be a better life for our kids than living in a big city like London. And it is beautiful and healthy here, with the sea and the sunshine. But sometimes strange things happen on Jersey, like this business with the dogs."

"Gee, I never felt anything strange about this island, until now," he told Mrs. Thompson. He put down his drink. "I'd better get going and try to find our dogs before it gets late. Thanks for the lemonade, and don't worry. I'm sure there's a logical explanation for everything that has happened." David got up and Mrs. Thompson walked him to the door.

"Thank you, David," she said. "Please, if you find out anything, even bad news, let me know."

"I will, Mrs. Thompson. I promise."

David rode off on his bike, puzzled about the problem. It didn't make sense. There was no pet shop on Jersey that would buy stolen dogs. Who would want them and where could they be?

David remembered reading somewhere that

some cultures considered dogs and cats tasty food, but he doubted that any people like that lived on the island. He was much more worried about disease. What if there was some sort of dog disease on the island, like that "mad cow" disease he had been hearing so much about? If the disease was deadly enough, it could kill off the dogs before anyone really knew what happened. He was tempted to go to the island vet, but then thought better of it. If there was a "mad dog" disease on the island, he would have heard about it. And anyway, there were still plenty of dogs on the island and none of them looked sick.

David didn't think Rusty could find his way to Fort Regent and, if he did, the guards at the fort would never let him in, so he decided to search in the area of the German Underground Hospital.

The hospital was carved out of a wall of rock. The tunnel that led through the entrance was grim and ominous looking. A plaque on the wall leading into the hospital read:

Under these conditions, men of many nations labored to construct this hospital. Those who survived will never forget. Those who did not will never be forgotten.

David shivered. The place was very scary. It had been built by forced labor. The men had constructed nearly a mile of corridors and chambers out of the rock, so that German soldiers in the underground hospital would be safe from bombs falling from Allied planes. The workers had removed 43,000 tons of rock and they had poured 6,000 cubic meters of

concrete. The hospital could take care of 500 patients and it was gas-proof, heated, and air-conditioned. There were operating theaters, staff quarters for the doctors and nurses, and offices, as well as stores.

David tagged along with a group of tourists. The tour guide was giving a detailed explanation of how well the German soldiers were taken care of in the hospital as compared with the gruesome existence of the Allied soldiers forced to work under terrible conditions.

The tourists walked into a different room and suddenly it became very quiet around David. He closed his eyes for a moment, trying to imagine what the laborers had been through, when he heard very faint barking. He put his ear to the wall and heard the barking even stronger.

Rusty! he thought to himself.

David rushed to the front office where a volunteer, an old man, was puttering about. "Do you have a plan of this hospital?" he asked excitedly.

"I certainly do, lad. I was one of the engineers who was forced to build it for the Germans." He went to a cabinet and took out a large plan all rolled up and now yellowed with age. "Do you want to have a look at it?"

David nodded. The man rolled out the plan and showed David where they were in the plan.

"See how the tunnels actually run into some of the outlying streets of the city? The Germans were

afraid of the Allied bombing and tried to keep underground as much as possible."

David traced some of the long passages with his finger. He was amazed to see that one of them began in a lane off Aquila Street, where Mr. Heinrich lived.

With a quick "thank you," he ran back to where he had left his bike and began pedaling furiously until he reached Heinrich's cottage. He could see the old man in the kitchen, cleaning up some dishes. David hid in the bushes, waiting to see if Mr. Heinrich would leave. Before long he saw Mr. Heinrich leave the house, heading towards town.

The kitchen door was unlocked, so he let himself in. He tried to find some sort of basement or staircase leading beneath the house, but there didn't seem to be any lower floor. He was about to give up hope when he remembered what the Glickmans had told him about the fierce storms that occasionally buffeted the island.

"Everyone is required to have either a basement or some below-ground room in case of hurricane winds," Mr. Glickman revealed. "You and I are sitting on top of a door I had built into the floor that goes into just such an emergency room. We've got food and water down there for at least a week."

David looked around, paying close attention to the floor in the living room. He saw a large throw-rug in the middle of the floor. Sure enough, when he pushed it aside, he discovered a trap door. When he raised the door, there was a flight of steps going down.

It was dark, too dark for him to wander down without knowing what waited beneath. He ran into the kitchen and searched through the cabinets until he found a flashlight. He beamed the light down the stairs, but still couldn't make out the floor at the bottom.

What if Mr. Heinrich returns when I'm down there? he thought. He didn't think the favors he had done for the old man would count for much if Mr. Heinrich thought he was snooping.

"Maybe I should tell Mr. Glickman what I've found out," he said out loud. But then he heard the familiar bark of Rusty coming from somewhere beneath him. Without hesitating, he began the climb down the staircase, leaving the trapdoor open.

As he climbed lower he began to hear the barking of many dogs. He could just make out Rusty's whine above the others.

When he reached the bottom, he shined his flashlight in front of him. There was a tunnel leading off from the little room he was in. He followed the tunnel and heard the barking of the dogs getting louder and louder. There was a little bend in the tunnel. He knew what he would find when he turned the bend, but just then he heard a loud "Mein Gott!" as the trap door slammed shut.

It was too late to turn back, and he knew Mr. Heinrich was probably making his way down the steps at that very moment. So, David rushed forward.

23

A bright light blinded him for a moment. He was in a small, stone room. There were cages on metal shelves all around the room. And in almost every cage there was a dog. Some of the dogs barked ferociously, others seemed to whimper and cry. Still others lay very still, as though they didn't have the strength to emit even a single sound.

In a flash, David found Rusty. He unlocked the cage and Rusty jumped into his arms. The room was damp and chilly and David could feel Rusty shivering in his arms.

"Here I am, Rusty," David whispered. "I've got you now, boy. Don't worry. No one is going to hurt you anymore."

David was about to release Susy, whom he spotted crouching quietly in a cage much too small for her, when all the dogs starting barking and growling in unison.

"Vaht you do!" A voice shouted at him. "Gib me back my dog!"

David turned around and saw the old man standing at the entrance of the room. He was carrying his walking stick. David squeezed Rusty tighter.

The other dogs were now howling and barking wildly. David could barely hear Mr. Heinrich.

"Gib me back my dog!" the old man repeated, raising his walking stick, menacingly.

"No," David answered. "This is my dog, Rusty. You know that, Mr. Heinrich. He's been here with me many times. Remember, we're the ones who helped you when you were hurt."

Mr. Heinrich looked at David for a long time. The dogs quieted down. David was wondering if he could make a run for it, push the old man aside, and climb up the stairs. Maybe even lock him in.

But as he looked at Mr. Heinrich, he realized that the man wasn't going to hurt him. He looked more stooped than ever before. And slowly, as he lowered his walking stick, David saw that the man was crying.

Mr. Heinrich began talking, first in German, and then, noticing that David was there, in his broken English.

"I young man when Nazis take this island. I just soldier, listen to orders, but see much. I belong to dog unit. Special dog unit. I like dogs then. Dey like me. I teach dogs be guarding against British. Against Americans. My commandant say I good soldier. Teach dogs vell.

"I teach dogs to attack enemy. But then the commandant get new orders. Terrible orders. Orders I no can believe."

Now Mr. Heinrich started to cry. He leaned against the opening of the room but David rushed forward thinking that the old man might fall. He tried to hold him with one hand and Rusty with the other.

"No, you not understand!" Mr. Heinrich yelled, tearing himself away from the boy.

"The dogs! They are evil! Terrible dogs! Giant schnauzers, shepherds, rottveilers, alsatians, and

dobermans. My babies that I train to protect us. My commandant vants that I should use them to attack the prisoners, to teach dem lessons, not to escape. I say no. I vill not use my babies to kill prisoners. Verbotten! Not permitted.

"My commandant say I am bad soldier. He puts me in jail. But Allies come and bomb island, bomb jail. I run away. No one find me in tunnels. Never in tunnels. When Nazis leave I stay. I stay and people remember. I not kill prisoners."

David finally understood.

"But then, you didn't do anything wrong. So why are you doing something wrong now? What do you plan to do with all these dogs?"

As though not hearing him, the old man continued.

"Der dogs, dey rip soldiers to pieces. Dey kill. My babies told der prisoners are bad and dey moost kill them. For long time I dinka about dis. Den I understand. I understand," he said, shaking his head. "Dogs bad too. Dogs kill. No reason. Just kill. So I kill all the dogs." Mr. Heinrich looked up and pointed to the dogs in the cages. "I kill dem all."

"But how did you catch them all?" David asked. "Why would they come with you?"

The old man smiled.

"I learn many tricks. Many vays to make dogs do vhat I say. It easy. It my life for long time. I no forget. Sometimes I give food. Sometimes I play game. Sometimes I just talk to dog and dog listen. Dis ist vat I know."

David helped the old man up the stairs. He took Mr. Heinrich to his room and helped him lay down. The old man was mumbling in German, clearly living in a different world, filled with guilt that wasn't even his.

David used the phone in the kitchen to call his grandmother. She called the police.

The police arrived just as the Glickmans drove up with David's grandmother. Everyone rushed in at the same time. David showed the police where Mr. Heinrich was resting. Then he went downstairs with them to where the dogs were kept. The town vet was called and he looked over each dog, checking for disease and malnutrition.

Everyone treated David like a hero. And as each family was called to pick up their dog, they thanked David for what he had done. Mrs. Thompson gave him a big hug and made Susy give him a kiss on his cheek. David was a bit embarrassed. The Glickmans were crying with gratitude to have Rusty safely back and treated David like a hero.

An ambulance came to take Mr. Heinrich to the island hospital. But by the time the ambulance reached the hospital, Mr. Heinrich had passed away.

When David heard the news of Mr. Heinrich's death, he was sad. The old man had seen some terrible things during the War. He had thought he was doing his duty for his country, but his country betrayed him. However, instead of being angry at his

country, he decided to take it out on the one thing he really loved, his dogs.

"What a terrible way to spend your life," David told his grandmother as they were all recounting what had happened. "Hating the dogs he loved just made him crazy."

"Well, I think his death came at the right time," suggested Mr. Glickman.

"Can you imagine being an old man and being sent to prison?"

Everyone agreed, although David still felt very sad about it.

The local paper wrote up the story, and David was the hero of the day.

They made a big party for him at St. Helier's and interviewed him on television. All the people who had regained their dogs set up a Jersey branch of the Society for the Prevention of Cruelty to Animals, and they named it The David Society in his honor.

When he got home to New York with his grandmother, everyone asked about his summer. Eyes shining, David said: "It was the most exciting summer of my life. I want to go again next year to see Rusty and his owners, the Glickmans, of course." He kissed his grandmother. "Any time you want to visit old friends, you can count on me!"

TREASURE IN A TEAPOT

BY TOVAH S. YAVIN

About Tovah S. Yavin...

Tovah S. Yavin has published poetry for adults and children in magazines such as *Jewish Affairs, Horizon,* and *The Formalist.* She was also honored to receive the *Sydney Taylor Manuscript Award* from the Association of Jewish Libraries for her middle-grade novel, *All-Star Brothers.*

Mrs. Yavin lives in Columbia, Maryland with her husband, daughter, dogs, and cats, and frequently emails her sons who are away at college. She also treasures the beautiful teapot given to her a few years ago by friends who left Russia to discover their Jewish heritage in America.

TREASURE IN A TEAPOT

Miriam pushed a tall stack of books across the dining room table towards Vika. "These are for you," she said.

"This is for you," Mrs. Plotkin said.

Miriam might have thought she was hearing an echo if it hadn't been for the heavy accent.

She twisted around to look into the living room where her mother and Mrs. Plotkin were sitting together on the sofa. Mrs. Plotkin held out a small cardboard box. It had a grease stain on the front and one crushed corner.

Kind of a funny way to bring a gift. She turned back to Vika and forced a smile.

"They didn't know what math you were ready for, so they put you with me. But I'm in the advanced class, so that's just going to be in the beginning while I'm showing you around. Once you get to know how things work, they'll move you to the right class."

Vika nodded and Miriam wondered if she understood a single word.

"Rabbi Kaplan is going to meet with you for Hebrew. He sent this." She pointed to the small Alef-Bet book at the bottom of the stack.

"Oh, Polina! Really. I can't."

Miriam turned around again. She watched her mother lift a teapot out of the cardboard box, hold it high, and turn it slowly this way, then that way. It was funny looking – chunky and fat. And it had orange

and gold flowers that were way too brightly painted all around its great, plump middle.

But the worst part of it was the lid. It had a kind of curlicue sticking up in the air. Miriam tried not to smile. She wouldn't want to embarrass their guests.

"So, here's your schedule," she said, turning back to Vika. "This is the room number and this is...."

She looked up and realized that Vika wasn't listening to her. Instead, she was staring over Miriam's shoulder into the living room, her eyes fixed on that ridiculous teapot. It seemed to Miriam that if she had to bring all of Vika's school things to her, lead her around for the first week, and miss the skating party today, then Vika should at least act like she cared.

"I'm getting some lemonade," Miriam said with a sigh. "Want some?"

Vika answered in Russian. That's what Miriam thought at first. Then she realized that Vika was actually talking to her own mother in a low, tight voice. Miriam didn't need to know Russian to sense that Vika was angry. Mrs. Plotkin just looked up, glared at her daughter, and put a finger to her lips.

"So do you?" Miriam persisted. "Want some lemonade?"

Vika finally focused her attention on Miriam. "Oh. Yes. Thank you."

By the time Miriam returned, however, Vika and her mother were saying their goodbyes.

Miriam left both lemonades on the dining room

table and dashed for the phone. Maybe she could still catch a ride to the skating rink.

The next day at school, Vika followed Miriam around like a kid sister. Miriam didn't so much mind leading her to her classes, but she would have liked to have been able to at least spend lunch with just her own friends. And anyway, everybody wanted to talk to Vika the whole time.

The girls wanted to know what Moscow was like. How long was the plane ride to America? What did other Russian people think when they heard that the Plotkins were leaving? Did they think that was a terrible thing to do?

"No," Vika answered. "People wished us luck, and said they were sorry that they weren't leaving, too."

And how did she know so much Hebrew? All the girls wanted to know that because when they heard that a Russian immigrant would be joining their freshman class at the Yeshiva High School for Girls, they all thought she wouldn't know an aleph from a bet. After all, they had heard about how the Jews in Russia had not been able to practice their religion at all for so many years. But Vika did know Hebrew and Rabbi Katz decided to put her in the middle group, which was also Miriam's class.

"So how did you learn so much Hebrew?"

Miriam asked, while they waited for their ride at the end of the day.

"My brother, Micha, had bad time in school," Vika answered quietly. "Boys always mean to him because we are Jewish. But we hardly know what that means. And we don't understand because we live like everybody else. Then a Yeshiva came to Moscow. So, he went two years. At night, he teach me."

"But didn't you have your own homework to do?"

"Yes. Lot of homework. But my brother tell us we need to know to be Jews. Is important. My mother and father were too busy. So I learn."

Miriam's mother arrived to pick up the two girls. She had volunteered to give Vika rides to and from school so that Vika could attend the same Jewish girls' school that Miriam attended. She had also suggested having Vika stay at their house every afternoon until Mr. Plotkin could pick her up.

Miriam's mother had done the volunteering, but it was Miriam who had to actually spend the time with Vika.

"We can do our homework here." Miriam led Vika to the dining room and dropped her books on the table, with a clatter.

Behind the table was a large display case. It had an entire shelf of candlesticks, another of spice boxes, and many of Mom's favorite items, including a silver goblet that had been a wedding gift.

On the middle shelf, prominently displayed, was the fat, ugly teapot that Mrs. Plotkin had given

them.

Vika spotted it right away. She gasped, then covered her mouth as she slid into a chair and opened one of her books.

Both girls started to work on their algebra problems. The first one was hard. Miriam tried it three different ways and couldn't get the answer shown in the back of the book. She looked over at Vika's paper and saw that she was already on the fourth one. That was very annoying, so Miriam went to the kitchen to get some snacks.

When she came back, Vika was standing in front of the display case, reaching for the teapot.

Miriam set the dish of snacks down on the dining room table and Vika jumped.

"Oh! You so quiet. I was just – " Vika's face turned a bright red. "Umm...I was...I was...."

"It was very nice of your mother to give us that," Miriam said, pointing to the teapot.

"This. Yes. We had in Russia. My mother very grateful for your family's help. I mean, we all are."

Then there was silence. Vika looked down at her book and papers, but seemed unable to move away from the teapot. Miriam felt awkward, too, and decided it was time to talk about something else.

"It doesn't look like you're having any trouble with these problems."

"No. I learn in Russia, already. I can help," Vika said, pointing to Miriam's paper.

They both sat down again and Vika showed Miriam how to do the problems. Her way made it easy to solve the problem. After Vika did two of them, Miriam got the idea and had no trouble doing the rest. They both finished early, so Miriam suggested that they watch television until Mr. Plotkin arrived.

Vika slipped away to use the bathroom. She was gone so long that Mr. Plotkin had already arrived to pick her up, just as she was joining Miriam on the sofa again.

As soon as she left, Miriam's mother wanted to know everything. Did Vika have any problem finding her classes? Did she get along with the other girls?

"It was kind of annoying though," Miriam added after answering Mom's questions. "I never got a minute to myself. No one even bothered to talk to me today."

"Well, Vika's new and different." Mom handed over a stack of dishes and motioned for Miriam to begin setting the table.

"I know. I know. She seemed, well, a little lost."

"I can understand that."

"And nervous."

Miriam set out the silverware that Mom handed her. Her glance fell upon the display case.

"This seems to make her as nervous as anything," she said, pointing to the tubby teapot.

"Do we really have to keep it here. It's so ugly."

"It's not really ugly. You think it's ugly? It's a different style than we're used to. I really didn't want to accept it. And not," Mom laughed, "because I didn't

36

like it. I just know how little the Plotkins have now. It must have been hard for them to give this away."

Miriam thought about that for a moment, then moved closer for a better look.

"Do you think it's some kind of heirloom or a valuable antique?"

"Well," Mom shrugged, "I'm guessing it was special to them. Think about it. They only brought a few suitcases with them. They didn't have room for much. They would have had to choose very carefully what to bring."

"And they chose this," Miriam ran her finger along the bulging teapot belly.

"They chose that." Mom nodded. "Then they gave it to us. That makes me feel that it's a very valuable gift."

"Hmm." Miriam examined the fake-looking gold paint on the teapot's lid. Or was it fake? "I have the feeling Vika thinks it's valuable, too. Did you notice how angry she got when her mother gave it to you?"

"Not really," Mom said.

"Well, I did. And then, when I stepped out for a minute this afternoon, I came back and found her over here, reaching for the teapot."

"That's funny," Mom paused to look at Miriam. "Because I came in here while you were watching

television and found Vika holding it. I guess I startled her because she got kind of flustered when she saw me."

"Yeah, and she got all blushy when I caught her reaching for it," Miriam announced. "Think she was trying to take it back?"

"Oh, certainly not. Vika wouldn't do something like that. Would she?"

Miriam just shrugged.

The next day in school, Mrs. Johnson asked Vika to speak to their history class about her life in Russia.

"M-my English not good," Vika stammered.

"That's okay. No one will mind," Mrs. Johnson reassured her. "Why don't you bring something to show? You won't even have to talk very much. Maybe, something special that you brought with you from Russia."

"You could show this pencil," Rebecca suggested as the girls sat around the lunch table trying to offer Vika ideas for what she could show. She picked up Vika's pencil, admiring the small doll head at the top where the eraser should have been.

"Is just a pencil."

"But it's different, isn't it?" Rebecca got agreement from all the girls at the table. "We've never seen a pencil like that. And it's pretty."

"But is not special," Vika insisted. She waited until she had a moment alone after lunch to tell Miriam what she did think would be special enough to bring.

38

"Would your mother let me borrow tea-pot?"

"I'll have to ask her," Miriam said, shoving one set of books into her locker while she pulled a different set of books out. "But I'm sure she'll say 'yes.'"

"Of course, you can borrow the teapot to bring to school," Mom told Vika that afternoon as the girls worked on homework at the dining room table.

"I have something to tell you," Vika whispered when the girls had the room to themselves again.

"About the teapot?" Miriam asked.

"Yes. How did you know?"

"Just something – doesn't matter."

"Is it valuable?"

Vika pulled her eyebrows together in a tight V.

"You know, worth a lot of money? My mother won't mind giving it back."

"No. No. My mother would never take back. I don't think it is much money. That not problem. It is message."

"Message?"

"From my grandmother."

"I don't think I understand."

Vika answered with a shrug. "When we are packing, my mother say bring only what we need. There is so little room. We give so much away."

"That teapot must have taken up a lot of room."

"My grandmother want me to take it. My

mother say no. But my grandmother say we must take. Then, just before we leave, she tell me teapot has important message. I will understand in America."

"And do you understand?"

Vika shook her head from side to side.

"But why would your mother give it away then?"

"My grandmother tell only me."

"So, it's a message?" Miriam said, gently lifting the teapot. "Does that mean there is something written on it?"

"I never look." Vika bent close, as Miriam turned the teapot, slowly. "So much happen and I forget until I see that my mother give away."

The girls examined it carefully. There was no writing on it anywhere. Not even "Made in Russia" on the bottom. Miriam lifted the lid by its curlicue handle to see if anything was written underneath it.

She almost didn't notice the dark velvet cloth tucked deep inside the pot. She tilted the pot for Vika to see, then waited for her to lift out the soft cloth. Vika slowly unfolded it, revealing a small square of thick paper. She turned the paper over and saw that it was a photograph. The picture was probably black and white at one time, but now it was more gray and yellow. There was a zig-zaggy crack running through it and the edges were frayed. The image of a man with a long, gray beard and wearing a stiff, dark hat stared grimly back at the two girls.

"Who is that? Do you think your grandmother

put that in there?"

"I don't know."

Vika looked at the picture for a long minute. She turned it over, and Miriam noticed some faded writing on the back that she recognized as Russian.

"What does that say?"

Vika stared at it, then held it up to the light. "It is so hard to read. This say 'Moscow.'" She pointed to one word. "And this is a date, but I can only see the '18.' The rest I see some letters but it is too light to read."

"I'll bet it's a name. Do you think he's a relative of yours?"

"Tonight, we call my grandmother," Vika said as she carefully tucked the picture into her bookbag. "I will ask."

The next day at school, Miriam tried to get a moment alone with Vika. But Vika seemed too busy to talk. She spent all of first period writing in her notebook. Miriam watched her write furiously, then scratch out line after line just as furiously.

When the bell rang, Vika wadded up the page of notes and dropped it into the garbage on her way to second period. She filled up more pages during that class and threw them away, too. Vika passed Miriam a note during third period. It had one sentence:

"What I should say in History class?"

41

Miriam shrugged. Then, she wrote:

"Don't worry. Anything is okay."

When it was finally time for Vika's talk, Miriam watched her walk slowly toward the front of the room. Vika turned to face the class, and Miriam gave her a most encouraging smile.

"This is teapot we bring from Russia," Vika began. "It belong to my grandmother, then she give my mother on wedding. We use when visitors come."

Rebecca raised her hand. "Can you pass it around," she asked. "We'll all be careful with it."

Vika handed the teapot to the girl closest to her, swallowed, and went on.

"We don't have many visitors in Russia. People know we are Jewish, and they don't come. Just my family. Some friends. They are Jewish, too."

"But why would they care?" Rebecca asked without bothering to raise her hand. "I mean, if they were just coming for a tea party, why would it matter?"

"People in Russia afraid. After my parents make papers to leave, even our family afraid. We talk on telephone, but they don't come."

Vika took a deep breath, while the girls in the class waited quietly. Miriam wished she could do more than just smile for Vika. Then, there was a tap on her shoulder from behind and it was her turn to look at the teapot.

She had already seen it up close, of course, but now she really noticed the flowers painted all around it. Every one was different. There were straw-

berries along the bottom and a butterfly peeking out from behind one blossom. Miriam guessed it had been hand painted. The curlicue lid had an elegance to it. Somehow, the teapot seemed much prettier now than it had at first.

"Is different here," Vika continued, drawing Miriam's attention away from the teapot. "Here we have friends already. And people come to visit at our house." She looked over at the teacher.

"That is all I can think to say."

"That was wonderful, Vika. Thank you so much for sharing this beautiful teapot and telling us about Russia. I think we all learned a lot. Didn't we class?"

Vika slipped back to her seat. Miriam suddenly remembered that she hadn't had a chance to find out if Vika knew anything more about the picture that they had found. She tried to ask her during lunch, but that proved hard to do. All the girls wanted to talk to Vika about her life in Russia and everyone wanted another chance to see the teapot. Finally, during an afternoon break, Miriam pushed through a crowd of girls to grab Vika by her sleeve.

"I want to show you our library," she announced, dragging her away from the other girls.

"Okay," Vika answered slowly.

Miriam pulled Vika into the library and maneuvered her behind a large bookcase. Then she switched to a whisper. "What did you find out? About

the picture?"

"I'm not sure."

"But you asked, didn't you?"

"I only talk to my grandmother for a few minutes. My father worry how it costs. So I tell her about school and about you," Vika smiled.

"About me? You mean about all of us at school?"

"Well, mostly just you." Vika looked off in the distance. "I tell how you teach me to be American."

Miriam could feel her face growing hot. She hurried to change the subject. "But didn't you ask her about the picture?"

"I ask when my father go out of kitchen. I tell her I find picture but don't know who it is."

"What did she say?"

Vika slid down into a nearby chair.

"She cried."

"Your grandmother cried?"

"She say is her father. But, she cry and I could not hear very well. Her father tell her never lose this."

"The picture, you mean? She wasn't supposed to lose the picture?"

Vika shrugged. "Her father tell her this is what we are, and no one can take away."

"But, that doesn't make sense. How can a picture be what you are?"

"I do not understand, either. But my grandmother cry. And then my father come in, and I must hurry because the phone cost so much."

There was a rustle of papers from the other

side of the room, then the tap of footsteps.

Miriam put a finger to her lips, and Vika nodded. The girls waited silently as the footsteps came closer and closer.

"Hello, girls." Mrs. Katz, the librarian, peeked around the bookcase with a smile. "I thought I heard someone come in."

"I was just showing Vika – "

"Were you looking for books about Russia?" Mrs. Katz interrupted, pointing to the stack of books next to them.

Miriam looked up and realized that they were surrounded by history books.

"Let me show you where they are." Mrs. Katz headed down the aisle and the girls followed.

"Mrs. Johnson said you gave a wonderful talk, Vika. Maybe, sometime, you can speak again for all the teachers. I think you can help us all to understand better what it is like to live somewhere very different. Here you are." Mrs. Katz pointed them to several shelves of books about Russia, then left them alone.

"When can you talk to your grandmother again?"

"My father worry about the money. He say next month, maybe."

"Next month! But what about the message? Is it just supposed to be the picture? I'll die if I have to

45

wait!"

Vika had taken a book off the shelf and was flipping through it. She paused at one page to examine a photograph. "I've been here." She held up the book for Miriam to see.

"Are you homesick?"

"Home? What you say? Sick?"

"Homesick. Not sick. You know, like you miss being in Russia."

"I miss my friends. I miss my grandmother." Vika looked up with a slight smile. "I am happy to be here."

Miriam reached for Vika's hand, just as the bell rang. "I guess we'd better go. We'll be late."

Miriam turned to leave, but Vika paused.

"Can I borrow these books?"

"Sure. Pick what you like."

Vika quickly picked out a few books about Russia and the girls hurried on to class. Miriam noticed that Vika stayed to herself for the rest of the afternoon. Every time she looked, Vika had her nose in one of the books about Russia. Miriam suspected she would feel the same if she had left everything and everyone that she'd ever known, to go someplace completely new.

They talked little the rest of the day, even in the car on the way to Miriam's house. Vika waited until they were both settled in the dining room, with their homework spread across the table, to show Miriam what she had found.

"Read this," she said, pushing one of the li-

brary books over to Miriam.

Miriam read for a while. The doorbell rang and Vika started gathering her papers together to go home. She paused for a moment, as she happened to glance towards the display case. Then she stepped closer to examine an object on one of the lower shelves.

"What is this?" she finally asked, pointing to a candleholder with many branches.

"That's a menorah. For Hanukkah," Miriam answered. "Didn't you ever celebrate Hanukkah?"

Vika shook her head.

"Well, it's kind of a complicated story. You'll hear all about it in a few months when it's Hanukkah time. But anyway, it lasts eight days and you light candles each day. This is where you put the candles."

"I see a picture like this, before."

"You've seen a picture of a menorah?" Miriam repeated.

"Not a picture on paper. A picture on something metal. Something small. Like this." Vika held her fingers about four inches apart. "This big with a picture like that." She pointed to the menorah. "What you think is?"

"What do I think it is?" Miriam paused to nibble at her lower lip as she tried to imagine what Vika could be describing. "Something small with a picture of a menorah. Was it jewelry? A necklace?"

"Maybe. I don't think so. It did not have chain."

"Well, let me see it."

"I don't have. My grandmother show me once. A long time ago. She said it should be mine. My grandmother talk like it was very special. But, I was little and I only like toys then."

"I know what you mean," Miriam laughed. "When I was little I only liked toys, too."

"I think she forget," Vika went on. "That it should be mine some day. I just remember now when I see this, um – "

"Menorah," Miriam helped her out. "Well, let me think about that thing that your grandmother showed you. I'll try to figure out what it could have been."

The girls said goodbye, and Miriam went to find her mother as soon as Vika had left. She told her about the picture that they had found hidden in the teapot and how her grandmother had cried when Vika tried to ask about him.

"But you know what we found in a library book?"

"What?" Mom asked, turning away from the stew she'd been stirring.

"There were pictures of great synagogues in Russia. And Torahs and everything. I didn't think the Russian Jews had any of that."

"Well, that's true now," Mom said. "But it wasn't always true."

"And Vika didn't even know about Hanukkah."

Mom answered with a sigh. "It's terrible when

48

people are afraid to keep their own traditions and beliefs."

"Well, I'm awfully glad Vika's family found their way here. And I'm glad that they can live as Jews now."

"Me too," Mom said, ruffling Miriam's hair.

Miriam was quiet through dinner and, later, found it hard to concentrate on her schoolwork. She wandered into the kitchen for a glass of water just as her mother was hanging up the phone.

"There's going to be a party Saturday night," Mom told her. "Kind of a housewarming for the Plotkins, after Shabbos."

"Mmm. That's nice."

"Everyone is bringing them gifts. Household things. Since they brought so little with them...."

"Really? Maybe I could bring something for Vika?"

"You don't have to. Dad and I will be bringing something nice for the family."

"I know. But I think I'd like to. You know, at first I felt, well, a little thrown together with Vika. Like I was being forced to be her friend. But she really is nice. And I really do like her."

"I'm so glad to hear that, honey." Mom gave Miriam a quick hug.

Miriam got on the phone with all her friends to decide on a great gift for Vika. They agreed to pool

their money for a tape player and some music tapes.

But Miriam wasn't satisfied. She needed to give Vika something else. Something to show her that they really were going to be special friends.

She thought about it all evening and could come up with nothing. Not a single idea. Finally, she sat down at the dining room table with the teapot. It was supposed to be some kind of message for Vika. Miriam stared at it, hoping that it would give her a message, like the perfect gift to bring Saturday night.

She could think of nothing. Miriam ran her fingers along the side of the teapot feeling the tiny bumps and ridges of the painted flowers. She let her hand follow the shape of the curlicue lid.

She peeked inside the now-empty teapot and thought of that stern looking great-grandfather, and of all those wonderful synagogues that nobody had used for so long.

Miriam could think of a million things to give Vika. But none of them would say how glad she was that they had met, and how much she hoped their friendship would grow.

Then, she glanced at the display case and suddenly noticed the velvet cloth that they had found inside the teapot. They had forgotten about it. Mom must have tucked it into the corner of the shelf. Maybe Vika would like to keep it.

Miriam leaned back in her chair to reach for the cloth. It was just a little out of her reach and she only managed to grasp it with her fingertips, just enough to sweep it off the shelf, sending it fluttering

to the floor.

It landed with a thud.

How could a velvet cloth land with a thud? Miriam picked it up and felt something hard in one corner. It took a bit of searching for her to find the opening in one seam.

She pushed her finger into the small pocket sewn into the cloth and pulled out the object that had made the clanking sound. It was just as Vika had described it – shiny metal, about four inches long, and it had a delicately etched picture of a menorah on the front.

Miriam thought about calling Mom, but she didn't. She held the menorah up to the light and admired the delicate filigree work. A chill ran through her as she imagined all the hands that had touched this before her and what it must have meant to them. Then she remembered something.

What had Vika said about last night's phone call? The picture had turned out to be Vika's great-grandfather. The father of Vika's grandmother. And what had he said? *Never lose this because this is what we are.*

Now Miriam understood. And she knew that it was up to her to help Vika understand, as well.

The party on Saturday night was great, with food, music, and lots of gifts. The adults spent most of the evening in the kitchen, showing the Plotkins

51

how to use all of their new appliances. There was a microwave, a toaster, a can opener, and a waffle iron. Micha pushed their new vacuum cleaner all around the house, and Vika listened to all of her new tapes.

Then, the Rabbi brought out his own gift – a new mezuzah for the Plotkin's front door. Micha proudly explained to his parents that a mezuzah contained a parchment with words from the Torah. Every time they came through their door, it would remind them that they were Jewish.

The mezuzah that the Rabbi brought was held in a beautiful olivewood case, about six inches long.

The Rabbi asked Mr. and Mrs. Plotkin if they had ever seen a mezuzah before, or understood what was inside it. They shook their heads.

"One of the prayers written on this parchment is called the 'Shema.' It is one of our most important prayers. It tells us to always remember that we are Jews. It tells us to teach our children about being Jews."

Miriam watched Vika as the Rabbi nailed the mezuzah to their doorpost. Then, when everyone had moved away, Vika stepped up for a closer look.

"I found it," Miriam said in a hushed tone. "Your grandmother had sewn it inside the velvet cloth." She handed Vika the small, silver mezuzah, with a picture of a menorah etched on the front of its case.

Vika held it gently.

"This is it. This is what my grandmother showed me. I remember it now." Vika looked up at

Miriam. "She didn't forget."

"No," Miriam answered in a hushed voice. "And I asked the Rabbi to look at the parchment on the inside. He said it is still kosher. All the writing is still very clear. Your grandmother must have taken good care of this for a long time."

"What the Rabbi said," Vika pointed to the mezuzah that the Rabbi had just put on their front door, "about the words in here telling us to always remember that we are Jewish. Do you think that is the message my grandmother wanted me to have?"

"It would be a beautiful message, wouldn't it?" Miriam answered.

"Maybe we could put this mezuzah on the door to my room."

Miriam agreed and they quickly asked the Rabbi to help them put it up. It looked beautiful on Vika's door, and the girls took a moment to admire it while all the adults were preparing to leave.

"I think you can tell your grandmother that this mezuzah is just where it belongs now," Miriam said as she and Vika hugged.

"And so are you."

THE CASE OF
THE LOADED DREIDLE

BY ELIOT FINTUSHEL

About Eliot Fintushel...

Eliot Fintushel lives by himself in Santa Rosa, California, where he writes stories and ponders the Fifth Question: "HOW CAN I MAKE THIS STORY DIFFERENT FROM ANY OTHER STORY?" His work can often be found in science fiction magazines and anthologies.

In 1999, Eliot was a finalist for the *Nebula Award for Science Fiction*.

For his "day job," Eliot performs shows for children, using masks, mime, and puppets. He has twice won the *National Endowment for the Arts'* award for solo performers.

Best of all, he is the proud Soccer Dad of teenaged daughter, Ariel.

THE CASE OF THE LOADED DREIDLE

S am's the name. *Dreidle's* the game. I spin hard and I spin true, and when I lay down my *gelt*, I expect a fair return. After all, look at the odds. Half the time you're gonna get something for your effort: *hay* or *gimmel* takes care of that. And the other half of the time, with *nun* or *shin*, the worst you can do is drop a penny. No, the only real losers at dreidle are the *shlemazels* who don't know when to quit, who lose penny after penny, pot after pot, begging for another turn when their pockets are empty and their faces are as long as Methuselah's side-curls.

Lila was one of those.

She was a compulsive dreidler. Her parents and mine were related somehow: third cousins on the father's side, once removed, with a side of fries and a medium cola to go – something like that. We saw each other a few times a year on the holidays. She wasn't bad to look at. Freckles. Pigtails. You know the type. She had a smile that could fricassee chicken, and when she walked down the street, boys bumped into things.

Not that I was personally interested, mind you. I'm immune to that sort of action. Only one thing interests a kid like me, and it's got four sides and spins. But sometimes life comes knocking on both sides of a fellow's door. It barges right in on you, knocks the dreidle out of your paw, and screams in

your face: *"Cherchez la femme!"* which is French for trouble.

It all started on a sunny day in August, during that long dry stretch between *Shavuot* and the High Holidays. Too hot to breathe. It was the kind of a day that makes you dream of school. I was sitting in my office, bored to the skull cap, when I heard a knock at the door. "Patsy, will you get that?" I shouted. Patsy's my secretary. I haven't got a secretary, actually, but I always shout that.

The knocking continued, and it was clear that Patsy wasn't going to budge, so I heaved myself up off the orange crate I use for a chair. My office is a corner of my father's garage – just until I win a few more big dreidle pots, you understand. "Wait a minute. Here I come."

The garage door ratcheted up to the ceiling. I squinted into the sunlit drive – and my blood turned to *gefilte fish* gel. It was Melvin the Grip, the sorriest imp of a marble-hustling *gonif* you ever tripped over, and he was packing heat: I could see the slingshot sticking out the back pocket of his brown corduroys. Melvin was Big Harry Zots' strong-arm.

"Sammy, we need to talk."

I started to protest, but Melvin's eyes hardened, his lips narrowed, and he fingered the scrap of inner tube trailing out of that back pocket. I remembered the shiner that Johnny Metzger sported

after a certain little "chat" with Melvin, and Johnny was a seventh-grader with muscles like a braided *challah*. I let Melvin in.

He pushed past me as if he owned the place. In the looks department, Melvin was about as different from me as a blintz from a chicken. I've got curly brown hair, a ruddy complexion, and lips the size and color of a beet slice floating in *borsht*. Melvin was pale as gefilte fish, with a crewcut and lips like piano wire. He was four inches shorter than me, but all steel and brick. It was rumored that Melvin had a sense of humor, but that it was on extended vacation in New Zealand. His face was as tight as a bunched hanky, and when he talked, he kept his teeth clamped. If you let your mind wander, it was easy to picture your flesh between Melvin's incisors.

"Sure. Come on in, Mel, my man. Sit anyplace. The ping-pong table's okay. Or the pile of tires over there. The orange crate? No sweat. Good choice. So, what's on your mind, pal?"

"A certain acquaintance of mine is being inconvenienced, so happens, by a certain acquaintance of yours. My acquaintance is holding a quantity of your acquaintance's IOUs, which your acquaintance has been, shall we say, loath to honor. My acquaintance does not like being inconvenienced, if you catch my drift. And if you don't catch it, Sammy, believe you me, you will in a day or two, unless my

59

acquaintance is reconvenienced."

"I beg your pardon?"

"Darn it, Sammy, what's the point in me memorizing these *spiels* if you're not going to pay attention? Now I have to start all over. A certain acquaintance of mine...."

"You mean Harry Zots?"

"Of course I mean Harry Zots. Who else would I mean, the Queen of Sheba?"

"But who's my 'acquaintance,' the one who owes him money?"

"Your cousin Lila – where was I? A certain acquaintance...."

"She's not my cousin."

"Regardless, you don't want she should get a free face lift, do you? Courtesy of Big Harry? Because when Big Harry lifts 'em, boychik, they lick their foreheads at meal times. A certain...."

"But I haven't seen her in months."

"Well, see her. Put her in the picture. Tell her Harry means business. Tell her that if she doesn't make good on those dreidle debts, there's a mouthful of knuckles in her future – and in yours. And you know how good Harry is with gizmos, Sammy – you might find a little surprise in your cornflakes one morning, or you might open your bedroom door and hear a funny little click, the last sound you'll ever hear. Catch my drift?"

"I catch your drift, Melvin." It was a nose-wrinkling drift. The Grip was not a frequent bather.

"Listen, Sammy..." Melvin the Grip slipped off

the orange crate and started toward me. I shrank back expecting one of his trademark *klops*. Instead, he laid his meaty paw on my shoulder. "Sammy, make sure and tell Lila that I'm only doing this because Big Harry's making me. And Sammy...."

"Yeah?"

"Off the record – do you think I stand a chance with Lila, a guy like me?"

"Sure, Melvin, sure. You're exactly her type."

He smiled so hard the little icicles of his canines poked down over his lower lip, and his face turned cherry red. "You really think so?"

"Absolutely. You two go together like salami and eggs."

Melvin allowed himself another flutter or two and then got back to business. "So you'll tell her about the IOUs."

"Sure. Yes. Okay. Definitely. I'll do my best."

"One more thing...." He grabbed my collar and I pictured my family saying *Kaddish* over my remains. "Don't tell Big Harry I screwed up the speech, okay?"

"Anything for a pal."

"I don't owe that *shmendrick* Harry Zots one red cent."

With freckles like that, how could you not

believe her? Lila had cheeks like candied fruit slices. And she smelled like *Manischewitz*. The scent of sweet wine followed her everywhere, and I am not the poetic sort, believe me. I had laboriously traced Lila through my network of sensitively placed underworld contacts – also, her family was in the phonebook – and we had arranged a meeting at the Carter Street Playground. Now she sat on a swing with a dreidle in one hand and my heart in the other. I stood in front of her, dodging her Adidas' now and then when she pumped.

"That's not the way Big Harry sees it," I said.

I had to squint to see her. The sun was relentless and bright. The grass was the kind of green that makes a kid want to roll down hills. Knee-biters choked the playground, throwing things and screaming.

Lila turned up her nose. "Did Melvin come to you with that 'my acquaintance, your acquaintance' cockamamie? I bet Harry wrote that out for him. Harry makes him do everything. Harry's a bully. You know Harry's a bully, don't you, Sammy?" Lila dug her sneakers into the dirt and stopped the swing an inch in front of me. We were momentarily enveloped in a cloud of dust, our own little world, just Lila and me. "Don't you, Sammy?" She stared straight at me and I felt my socks start to wilt.

"Tell me what happened."

She jumped off the swing and stalked away. I followed at her heels.

"There's nothing to tell. We played a little

dreidle. I beat the pants off him, and now he's angry, that's all. He's the one who owes me the gelt, two dollars, to be exact. You don't know him. He can't stand to lose. When Harry loses, there's no controlling him. There's no telling what he'll do to get even. That's what this is really about, Sammy. Harry trying to get even."

She stopped suddenly, and I nearly ran into her. She spun to face me and turned up the thermostat again, fluttering those cherubic lashes of hers, flicking those pigtails with deadly charm. "Say, Sammy...."

"Yeah, doll?"

"You think you might do me a little favor?"

"What exactly did you have in mind?"

She tugged at my collar – I kind of liked it; it was the same spot Melvin had tugged, but Melvin was a couple pigtails short of charming. "Do you think you could collect my two dollars from Harry, Sammy?"

"Absolutely."

"And, Sammy...."

"Yeah?"

"How about a few spins before you go?"

Four gimmels in a row. She was so attached to that prize dreidle of hers; she made me use another

one on my spins. It was her lucky dreidle, she explained. Lady Luck worked for Lila like the Grip worked for Harry Zots. She beat me to the tune of thirty-five cents, and that's not a tune I'm fond of. But what a way to go! I thought I felt her palm, the base of her thumb possibly, maybe even a knuckle or two, when I plunked the quarter and dime into Lila's little hand. She smiled, and I floated off toward the Zots estate to give that bully a talking to.

Big Harry's mother answered the door. It shocked me that he had a mother. It's a regular lesson in compassion, is what that is. I mean, if even a *meshuggener* like Harry Zots could have an actual female mother, someone who loves him, tucks his shirt in, washes behind his ears, the whole nine yards, then there's nobody on earth who isn't a little bit lovable. Even gym teachers.

"What's all the banging? You think my door is a chicken to slaughter? You're being chased by wild dogs and you want shelter? You have to make maybe a Number Two?" Mrs. Zots pushed past me onto the front porch and tramped down the steps. She was a short round woman in a polka-dot dress with a smell of fenugreek. She carried a purse over one forearm, massive and lethal, with enough hardware on it to furnish a missile silo.

"Well, I gotta go shop," she said without turning around. "I was just leaving. Harry's inside. It's him you wanna see, right? You working on a science project with Harry? He's always working on science projects."

"Something like that," I said. But she was gone. I moved into the living room and cased the joint. In my line of work a fellow can't be too careful. Hardwood floor: a head could split on that baby if fists should fly. Two windows: one of them open to the width of my hips – possible escape route in case of an altercation. The other one a huge picture window shut tight. If worst came to worst I could heave Zots through it onto the lawn. If I was strong enough to heave him. If he let me. If he promised not to hit me back. And if I didn't have to clean up the glass, which I hate.

On second thought, forget the picture window.

I was just about to inspect the moldings when I heard a pounding in the hall, then a gravelly voice: "Melvin, izzat you?"

"No such luck, Zots," I said.

Big Harry entered the room and froze. He just stood there, all five foot two of him, most of it shoulders and biceps, looking down at me with those snake eyes of his. I thought I heard something start to hiss and rattle, but it could have been a teapot. My life flashed before me.

At moments like this, a pro dreidler such as myself has to keep his wits about him. It's all too easy to give way to panic. Dreidling brings a person into the society of all kinds of unsavory individuals, especially when it isn't confined to Hanukkah. You

65

never know what sort of brutal situation you may end up in when pennies change hands and tempers flare. You never know when that big dreidle in the sky, the one with your name on it, is going to come up shin.

I felt my smile start to sag at the edges, and my forehead started to sweat. As subtly as possible I checked my shoelaces – tied and double-knotted – and made a rough estimate of the distance to the door behind me. I recalled taking five steps in, but that was walking; at a clip, I could likely make it in two. I hoped that Big Harry wasn't that fast.

"What's this all about, Sam?"

"Let's just say it's about a certain acquaintance, shall we?"

"You bring me the gelt from Lila?"

"Try again, big man."

"Melvin talked to you, right?"

"I don't scare easy, Harry. You better know that about me right from the start." I was shivering down to my *gatkes*. "I don't scare and I don't bargain. Not with deadbeats and thugs."

"Wait a minute. Did Melvin threaten you?"

"You could say that. You could also say that King Kong was a monkey."

"That *nudnik*! I told him...Listen, why don't you come in and have a ginger ale, Sammy? We can talk this out, you and me."

"Sure. Why not?" He gestured for me to go first down the little hallway into the kitchenette. "Nothing doing. You first." He shrugged and led the way.

He sat me down at the table, pulled a bottle of clear liquid from the fridge, and set out two plastic tumblers. Mine was a Mickey Mouse. His was a Simpsons. He filled both of them with the bubbling stuff, returned the bottle to the fridge, and sat down opposite me at the table, all just as casual as could be. I watched him like a hawk.

"Say, Big Harry, you mind if we trade tumblers? So happens I'm partial to the Simpsons."

"Whatever you say, Sammy."

We switched. Even so, I waited until Harry took the first sip, and when nothing happened, I took a pull of mine. Tasted like ginger ale, all right. It went down smooth and easy, and I started to relax a little.

Harry made little circles on the table with the base of his wet tumbler. "Look, I'm sorry about Melvin, Sammy. He gets a little carried away sometimes."

"Oh, yes? According to a certain informant of mine, you're the one who wrote out that little speech for him."

"Speech? I don't know what you're talking about."

"You can cut the baloney, Harry. I talked to Lila myself."

"And?"

"She spilled her guts to me, Harry. She sang

like a canary. She told me about the two bucks you owe her – and about you writing Melvin's little standup routine."

"Now wait a minute, Sammy." I could see he was starting to sweat as bad as the tumblers. I had a sweet little fantasy of making circles on the table with him. "I didn't mean for Melvin to really scare you. I just asked him for a little intercession, is all...."

"Intercession, huh?"

"Yeah, intercession. Is there an echo in here or something? I knew he and you lived on the same block, and I knew you were Lila's cousin or something. So I thought he could, you know, enlist your aid in getting the dough she owes me. Owes me, Sammy, not the other way around."

"So why the *megillah*? 'Your acquaintance, my acquaintance...!' And why was he threatening me, if you didn't tell him to?"

"You'll have to ask Melvin that."

"I will, Big Harry. Count on it. And I still don't buy your story about the dreidle debt. You got Lila's IOU to prove it?"

"Of course not, Sammy. I'm not saying that I won. Lila won. Won and won. That's the whole point."

"Look, maybe I'm a little *shikker* here, maybe there's something in this soda pop besides bubbles and sugar water, but isn't it the custom for the loser to pay the winner?"

"Not if the winner cheats."

I narrowed my eyes. I gritted my teeth. I fisted

my hands under the table. "What are you saying?"

"That dreidle, the one she tucks under her pillow at night and keeps with her from Hanukkah to Hanukkah – Sammy, that dreidle is loaded."

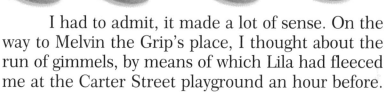

I had to admit, it made a lot of sense. On the way to Melvin the Grip's place, I thought about the run of gimmels, by means of which Lila had fleeced me at the Carter Street playground an hour before. You don't get that kind of action from an evenly weighted dreidle. Had she cheated me the way Harry said she had cheated him? Cheated and lied?

Dames.

I was in a spot now, a heck of a spot, having pledged each side that I'd collect from the other. Whoever won, Yours Truly would lose. But what about the Grip? Why had the messenger boy upped the ante without his boss's say-so – that is, if Big Harry hadn't lied to me about that. What was Melvin's angle?

The Grip was playing catch in his backyard with the only kid on the block who could stand his aroma – namely, himself. He stood in the petunias staring at the sky and holding aloft his catcher's mitt. The way he hefted that hardball, you'd have thought it would reach escape velocity and go into orbit. But

it kept coming back down all right, a regular meteorite: whump! Melvin's folks should have declared that backyard as a hard hat area and taken out extra insurance.

Only thing was, Melvin's father was vice president of the local garden club; if he knew Melvin was tramping on his petunias he would grind the Grip's *kishkes* and use them for fertilizer. I threaded between beds of Gloriosa Lilies and Royal Poincianas, pausing to enjoy the fragrance of a Chinese Hibiscus before braving the Grip's bouquet. I edged past the daffodils and tiptoed through the tulips, till I was standing a few feet behind Melvin. He still hadn't seen me.

I decided to use the element of surprise. "Nice day for it, eh, Grip?"

He turned suddenly, the ball hit him square on the noggin, and he fell like a loaded dreidle – only he wasn't coming up gimmel. "Ouch! Sammy, what's the big idea? I coulda got my brains ventilated."

"That isn't all that'll be ventilated if you don't come clean, Melvin. So happens I've just been chit-chatting with a certain acquaintance of yours, and guess what? He doesn't recall telling you to deliver any threats."

"Darn it, Sammy!" Melvin the Grip rubbed his head and laboriously stood up, uprooting a clump of prize gladioli. He was surrounded by divots the size of a foxhole, and a hanging basket of some kind of chrysanthemums was shards and roughage now.

"Darn it, I asked you not to tell Big Harry about

the speech, didn't I?"

"You asked me not to tell him you screwed up. I didn't. But I saw no reason to clam up on the whole business. What's the idea turning up the heat on Lila, if Big Harry didn't ask you to?"

Melvin stood there for most of a minute, ruminating on his shoe leather. Then he heaved a sigh and looked up. "You know I'm a goner for your cousin, Sammy."

"She's not my cousin, pal, but say I do. So what?"

"We had the same teacher last year, me and Lila. Well, ever since Valentine's Day, when she sent me that little card – 'Be mine,' it said, with a bunch of little hearts, the cutest reddest little hearts you ever laid eyes on, Sammy, so you knew they had to be sincere...."

"She must have given those things to everybody. You had Mrs. Tarbottom, right? She makes you give them to everybody."

"Mine was different, Sammy."

"Did it say 'Hallmark' on the back, by any chance? Was there a price sticker for fifteen cents?"

"Stop it. Mine was different, I tell you. Well, ever since then, I knew that me and Lila were meant for each other."

"Nu?"

"But then there was the Harry thing."

"What Harry thing?"

71

Melvin looked like he was about to say something important. Take it from an old dreidler, take it from a fellow who knows human nature like a *shochet* knows chickens, the bum was about to confess – something. Then, suddenly, he clammed. I could see the little marbles rolling around in his eye sockets, and when he finally talked, it was only to say, "Let's go see her, Harry. Let's go see Lila, you and me, together. Then you can ask her for yourself."

It was a tough call. Should I accompany the Grip to Lila's place or dump him and go by myself? He was holding back something – but what? I was starting to think that the whole thing was a setup, that Melvin was somehow in cahoots with Lila, and that nothing was what it seemed. "Why?" I asked myself. "Why? Why? Why?"

In my line of work a fellow learns one thing pretty quick: you can sing The Four Questions till you're blue in the face, but the answer will still be Hebrew. I helped Melvin repot the chrysanthemums, and we headed for Lila's, together.

Lila blocked the porch door. "It's not a good time, boys."

I wasn't in a mood for this sort of guff. The heat of the day was upon us now. Mosquitoes were playing knick-knack on my knee, and the sun was so bright you'd have thought the whole world was an interrogation room, and the sky was an angry DA.

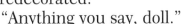

"Make it a good time," I said. "We've got a few things need talking over. Get the picture?"

"Sure, sure, I get the picture. Come on in, then. Cookies and milk?" She opened the screen door, and we pushed through. "Let's sit in the living room, okay? The kitchen's being redecorated."

"Anything you say, doll."

They were chocolate chip cookies – semisweet, like everything about Lila. I immediately sat down opposite her and shoveled two big ones into my mouth. The milk was cold and good and all milk, a real kid's drink, none of this 2% stuff.

Melvin remained on his feet. He kept fidgeting with the rubber on his slingshot. For the second time that day, I had the feeling that the Grip was holding something back.

At last, he broke out: "Ask her. Go ahead, Sammy. Ask her."

"OK, Grip." I turned to Lila. "A certain acquaintance of mine...."

Lila cut in, "You mean Melvin?"

"I am not at liberty to say."

She shot an angry look in the Grip's direction. "Melvin, you are such a nudnik. Why can't you speak up for yourself?"

Melvin blushed and said nothing. He considered his shoe leather again. I don't know what it was about that shoe leather.

"Ahem," I ahemmed. "As I was saying, Lila, this individual was describing to me a little Valentine's Day action he received vis-a-vis yourself. And in that context, my acquaintance made mention of some mysterious thing going on with you, Lila – a 'Harry thing,' he called it. My acquaintance has requested that I ask you about this matter in person. So I'm asking you, Lila, what is this 'Harry thing,' huh?"

"I don't know what you're talking about."

"You don't know what I'm talking about. Harry doesn't know what I'm talking about. Nobody knows what I'm talking about today. What, am I speaking Hebrew or something? Aramaic? Swahili? Lila, what is the 'Harry thing?'"

She stood up, nearly knocking her chair over behind her. "You two'll have to go now."

Why the sudden nervosity? I eyed the closed kitchen door. Redecorating, huh? "You wanna spin some dreidle, Lila? Why don't we just step into the kitchen and throw a few before we sashay out of here?" It seemed to be a day for kitchens. Noshing and kitchens. Could be worse.

"I told you we're redecorating."

Melvin exploded like a shook soda. "Harry's no good, Lila. He's a big bully. He threatened you. He threatened Sammy."

"You did that," she said.

"Harry made me. It was all Harry. He doesn't even really like you."

"Wait a minute," I said. "What's going on

74

here?" The air was burning between Lila and Melvin. They paid about as much attention to Yours Truly as a dinosaur to a gnat.

"Don't say that, Melvin." A softness crept into Lila's voice. Now she was the one taking in shoe leather.

"I'm the one who likes you, Lila. Not Harry – me." A sigh, then dead silence.

I ate another cookie. I watched the kitchen door.

"So the truth comes out," I said. "It seems the messenger boy doctored the message. You wanted to make Big Harry look bad, didn't you, Melvin?"

"Shut up." Now I was the shoe leather: Melvin looked at me as if he was about to give me a shine.

"You wanted to put the kibosh on the 'Harry thing,' isn't that right, Melvin? On the 'Harry and Lila sitting in a tree' thing, to be exact."

"Shut up, Sammy." Lila joined the chorus. She glared at me. Nobody seemed to appreciate the sound of my voice that day. Maybe I should take singing lessons, was my thought.

Before Lila realized what I was up to, I trotted past her to the kitchen door.

"Don't, Sammy, please!" Suddenly Lila was all scented hankies and flowers between the teeth. "You don't know what you're doing."

"Sure I do, sweetheart," I said. "I'm gonna turn the handle and shove."

And that's what I did, all right. Just as I had suspected, Big Harry Zots was standing inside. In his hand was Lila's dreidle. There was no mistaking that dreidle, a big plastic job with barber stripes on the handle.

You could have knocked Big Harry over with a feather. He just stood there, blushing. For the moment, I had the advantage, but I knew that if I didn't move quickly, I'd lose it. Big Harry would make a little calculation, and Little Sammy would receive an unsolicited facial: spell that k-l-o-p.

Sometimes I surprise myself. I grabbed the big dreidle right out of Harry's paw. "OK, Harry – talk." He just stood there looking back and forth between Melvin and Lila and me. He couldn't – or wouldn't – say a word.

"Everybody down on the floor," I said. And for some crazy reason they did it. I have tried to reproduce this effect numerous times since that day, but I have not been able to do it. When I order people around, they tend to do one of three things: ignore me, punch me, or laugh. This must have been one of my golden moments. Big Harry, Melvin the Grip, and Lila plunked themselves down in a neat little circle on the kitchen floor, and I squeezed in among them.

"Ante up," I said. Lila and Harry were too embarrassed to think, much less protest. The Grip was simply too stupid. They each threw two pennies into the middle – our accustomed ante. "I'll go first."

I spun.

Gimmel.

No one said a word. I raked in the gelt, we anted up again, and the Grip reached for the dreidle.

I grabbed his wrist. "Wait a minute. So happens Big Harry here has a theory about this dreidle of Lila's – don't you, Harry?" Silence. Shoe leather. "Anybody mind if I test it out?"

Once, twice, three times, I spun Lila's dreidle.

Gimmel. Gimmel. Gimmel. I collected the pennies.

I nodded slowly – something I saw John Travolta do in a movie once, and it made cornmeal mush out of Uma Thurman. I nodded and nodded. No cornmeal mush. I nodded anyway. "Seems like I'm having a run of luck here. What do you think, Lila? Shall I spin it again?"

She barely whispered, "It wasn't me, Sammy. I didn't load that dreidle."

Big Harry stood up in a huff. "I can't take it anymore. I'm the one who fixed Lila's dreidle. Yeah, I did it. Me, Harry Zots. And I'd do it again." He pulled a little gizmo out of his pocket, and I hit the deck, figuring I was dead meat. But instead of shooting the thing, he plunked it down in front of me and ran out of the room.

It looked like a remote control, the kind of gadget you run toy trucks and airplanes with. I picked it up. I fingered the little lever.

Lila blurted, "Don't...!"

But I pushed the lever home. Two feet away, the top of the dreidle popped off and out sprang a styrofoam ball with these words scrawled on it in fat red letters:

LILA –
I ♥ you.
– Harry

"Sammy, you fathead, you've spoiled everything." Lila shook like bullet-riddled glass, and her freckles danced the hanky panky. She showed me her teeth – a nice set, though I wasn't in the mood to admire it.

I eyed her coolly – Travolta couldn't have done it better. "You knew about the dingus."

"I knew there was something. Of course I did. It started last Hanukkah. My dreidle went missing while the Zots' were visiting. For half an hour or so, I couldn't find it – or Harry – anywhere. Then the dreidle turns up exactly where it's supposed to be, and there's Harry, wearing this silly grin.

"Ever since then, I can only get gimmels. I figure something must be up, but I can't quite figure it out. Who would suspect such a thing? I just thought my luck had changed."

"And then?"

"Then came the looks."

"Looks?"

"Yeah. Looks from Harry. Between classes at

school. Or when he walked by my house and I was on the porch – you know. Looks. Like Melvin's doing to me now."

I shot a glance at the Grip. He was staring at Lila. His face had turned to marmalade. His lip quivered. His eyes were oozing out of their sockets with a love light that can only be described as – yuchy.

"Okiedokie," I said. "All this I buy. The dreidle was loaded, but it was nobody's fault. The weight of the servo-mechanism that Big Harry stuck inside it happened to be just opposite the gimmel side. But why didn't Big Harry pop the love note on Hanukkah, when he loaded it there, instead of twiddling his thumbs for most of a year, and then letting me do it?"

"He was shy, you *schmendrick*. For most of a year, poor Harry beat around the bush. He acted funny. He couldn't get up the chutzpah. He was about to do it just now, but you had to spoil everything, bigshot detective, with your tough talk and your big nose."

"Big Harry shy?"

"Yes. He couldn't talk to me. He just kind of stammered and expected me to get the picture."

"The 'I heart you' picture, you mean."

"Exactly. Then he found another way of communicating."

"Let me guess. He picked a fight."

"Yes."

"I get it now. Tough guys in love: first they mumble, then throw spitballs."

"That's it. That's when the accusations began."

"He said you owed him money."

"Yes, and I said he owed me. That's when I started wondering about the dreidle. I held it up to the light. I really did win two dollars, you know. I didn't know till then that my dreidle was loaded."

"I believe you, Lila. So all the monkeyshines, the debts, the threats, the messages, me running around like a chicken with its head cut off, and Melvin here memorizing his two-bit monologues with the ten-dollar words, what it all boils down to is this: we were caught in the crossfire of a lovers' quarrel."

Lila blushed and smiled. "I guess you could say that."

I gave Patsy the day off and went over to Melvin the Grip's place to help him mend his broken heart. What are friends for, after all? I found him in the petunias, pulling weeds. I kneeled down beside him and started clawing up crabgrass.

"I suppose it's all for the best," he said.

"What do you mean, Grip?"

"If you hadn't gotten involved in this, if I'd taken matters any further..."

"Matters of the heart, you mean."

"Yes. If I'd pushed it, Sammy, I might have been sprouting petunias instead of weeding them."

"Hey, Big Harry's not such a mean guy. I don't take him for the jealous type, either. He wouldn't have hurt you, Grip, my man."

"Harry? Who's talking about Harry? Lila has the fastest left jab in the sixth grade."

"Anyway, there's plenty of fish in the sea. What about Miriam? Wasn't she in your class too?"

"The spelling champion, you mean? That Miriam? What makes you think she might like me?"

"She sent you a Valentine's card, didn't she?"

He stopped weeding and looked at me. His mouth dropped open. He stayed like that for a minute, catching flies, and then he broke out into the silliest grin I have yet witnessed on a human mug. "She did, didn't she?" He sighed. "Miriam!"

It put me in mind of dreidling again, of how you can hardly lose. I mean, it's only pennies, and the odds are pretty good. Look at Melvin. His dreidle had come up shin, so to speak. All that effort with Lila had gone to waste, yet here he was, anteing up all over again.

Miriam.

It gives a fellow pause.

Who Is Mrs. Schimer?

by Ellen Katz Silvers

דרכון

ישראל

About Ellen Katz Silvers...

I love writing! I write letters, lists, and, of course, stories. Since I was born and grew up in Wichita, Kansas, some of my stories, like *Who Is Mrs. Schimer?*, are based in the Midwest. Others take place in Arizona, where I lived for fourteen years. But my favorite place to write about is Israel, which has been my home since 1986.

My stories and articles have appeared in *The Jewish Observer, Horizons, More of Our Lives, People Like Us,* and *Fiction.*

I live in a small village, Shilo, where the Mishkan, the Holy Ark, once stood. My husband and our seven children all help me with my writing by listening, proofreading, and, most importantly, inspiring me with their kind words and helpful comments.

WHO IS MRS. SCHIMER?

Before my best friend, Cheri Cohen, moved away, she gave me some good advice: "Robin," she said, "You're one of the smartest girls in the school. Just let the kids from the other schools find it out for themselves and don't be bossy. They'll want to be friends with you, and you'll do fine in high school."

Cheri knew me better than I know myself, and her advice was good. Still, I sure was nervous about starting ninth grade in a huge school without a best friend. So, when Naomi Marcus moved to town in August, I thought my problems were solved. First of all, she moved in down the block from me and, second of all, she was Jewish. Not that my friends all have to be Jewish. In this town, most of them aren't. But it's nice to have a friend who understands my Jewish side and so knows the real me.

The Marcus family was from Israel, which I was dying to visit. But my mother kept telling me to wait until I was older. Well, at least I could have a friend from there.

Unfortunately, things don't always work out the way we think they should. The first week Naomi moved in, I went to her house to visit. Her parents and older sister were thrilled to see me, but not Naomi. I could barely get two words out of her. At first I thought it was because she didn't know English

85

well, but then I found out that she had lived in Chicago for two years before coming to Greenville, Illinois. Her English was fine. I decided right then and there that she was a snob. I mean, she had reason to be. She was gorgeous, with a good figure, long blonde hair, blue eyes – everything the opposite of me. No one was going to choose me to be their friend because of my looks.

School started and I ignored Naomi and made some new friends. They might not have been from the cool crowd, but they were nice.

Naomi, on the other hand, didn't make friends with anybody. And she had plenty of chances. During the first month of school, I overheard one of the most popular girls in the class ask her if she wanted to try out for the cheerleading squad. Instead of appreciating the offer, Naomi just shrugged her shoulders. Six months passed and she was just as much a loner as ever. So, when our ninth grade World History teacher paired up Naomi and me to do our World War II project, I wasn't pleased, to put it mildly. I was going to talk to Mrs. Graham about changing me, but before I could, Naomi approached me and asked if we could eat lunch together and talk about the project. How could I say no? Obviously, Naomi was being friendly so she could get a good grade, but I wanted a good grade too. We'd just have to work together the best we could.

"I think we should do our project about the Holocaust," I said emphatically as soon as we had found a table in the crowded lunch room.

"Yes," Naomi nodded thoughtfully, "but there is so much material for only twelve pages."

Only twelve pages! I thought twelve pages was incredibly long. But if you don't have any friends, I guess you have plenty of time for homework.

"Well," I drummed my fingers on the table. "We've agreed about the subject. What should we do with it?" I had an idea, but I didn't want to be too bossy.

"Maybe," Naomi played with her hair as she spoke, "we should take twelve different concentration camps and write a page on each."

I wrinkled my nose. "That sounds really dry. We'd just write about statistics. If we're the only ones writing about the Holocaust, and we probably will be, we have a responsibility to make it real, you know."

"Well, what do *you* suggest?"

"Maybe – " I hesitated for just a minute, "we can interview twelve different survivors. Their stories would be much more than statistics. We could write about their pains and losses and, in the midst of doing that, the statistics would come through." I was really excited about the idea.

"Are there twelve survivors living here in Greenville?" Naomi asked, slowly.

"Maybe not," I admitted, frustrated that she did not share my enthusiasm. "But use your imagination. We can make up interviews with

different people who wrote books about their experiences. And we can start with your grandfather's cousin."

Magda Schimer had moved to town to stay with Naomi's family two months ago, right before Hanukkah. I met her at the Hanukkah party at the synagogue and I liked her right away. She wasn't at all like Naomi. She was friendly and outgoing and, well, she reminded me of my grandmother. She even had the same hairstyle, dressed the same way, and had the same accent.

My *Oma* had come from Austria. She left when she was sixteen, before the war, and her English was perfect, but she never lost her accent. Maybe it's because she always spoke to my mother and me in German. She said she wanted us to have the advantage of knowing more than one language. I really miss her. She died right before my thirteenth birthday.

Apparently, Naomi liked my idea because she nodded her head and even smiled a little. She had a nice smile. "Okay, I'll ask Cousin Magda tonight."

"Great," I replied. "Call me as soon as you talk to her."

Naomi finally called right before I was going to bed. She said we could meet with her cousin right after school the next day. While we were on the phone, she filled me in on some of Mrs. Schimer's story. It was really interesting and I didn't know Naomi could talk so much. I couldn't wait to sit and talk with Mrs. Schimer.

I was surprised to find out that she and Naomi's grandfather were from Hungary, not Austria. Naomi's grandfather left their village not too long before World War II and made his way to Israel; it was Palestine then. I guess he understood that what was happening in Germany with Hitler and the  Nazis would sooner or later affect all of Europe.

Unfortunately, he was right. Hitler invaded almost every country in Europe and, in each country, he first sent all of the Jews to a ghetto, then to work camps, and then to death camps. Hungary was one of the last countries to be taken over, and by that time, Naomi's grandfather had already been in Israel for seven years. He tried to send for his parents and little sister, but he couldn't get permits from the British, who ruled Palestine then. Finally, the war ended, and he turned to the Jewish Agency to find out what had happened to his family.

It was so sad. They were all killed in death camps, or so he thought. Then, a couple of years ago, Magda Schimer contacted Naomi's father. She had never contacted him before. She had been saved by a Christian family and didn't even know that she was Jewish until she had grown up. However, once her husband died, she decided she wanted to find her real family. Naomi's father was the only relative she had left, so she went to Israel to be with him. Only, not long after she arrived, the family moved to

Chicago. She stayed in Israel for a while, but missed them, so she came to Greenville.

I still thought it was weird that Mrs. Schimer had the same Austrian accent as my Oma, if she was from Hungary. I planned to ask her about it.

When I arrived at Naomi's house the next day, Mrs. Schimer was really charming. And Naomi and I worked well enough together for her to think that we were friends. While we interviewed her, we nibbled on homemade butter cookies she had baked that morning. Too bad she didn't have any grandchildren.

We asked her some difficult questions. Here are a few of them:

> *How did the Nazis change your life?*
> *How many of your family members did you lose in the war?*
> *What is the last memory you have of your parents?*
> *What did you do after the war?*

Mrs. Schimer answered them all pleasantly, but her voice did get quivery when she told how her mother took her to their neighbor's house and told her she would be back soon. For days she would stand at the window waiting for her mother, but she never came. I had a lump in my throat and I looked over at Naomi and saw she was blinking back tears.

Then Mrs. Schimer said something kind of strange. She told us that the last relative she ever saw was Naomi's grandfather. Naomi didn't blink an eye

and just asked the next question. Her cousin told us that the end of the war didn't change anything for her. It wasn't until the night before her wedding that her foster parents told her the truth about her family and that she was really Jewish.

"You must have been in shock," I exclaimed.

"No, Robin," Mrs. Schimer shook her head. "I was in love, and all I cared about was my husband. It was after he died that I began to think about being Jewish and the Holocaust."

Just then the phone rang and Naomi jumped to answer it.

"Who was it dear?" Mrs. Schimer asked when Naomi returned to the room.

"I don't know." Naomi looked a little worried. "They hung up as soon as I said 'hello.'"

"Kids," Mrs. Schimer shook her head, impatiently.

"It's been happening a lot lately," Naomi informed her.

"I'll speak to your father. Maybe he should get an unlisted number."

"Maybe," Naomi agreed half-heartedly.

The phone rang a second time, and Naomi let it ring five times before picking it up.

This time it was a legitimate caller, my mother. She asked me to pick up milk on the way home, so that was the end of our discussion.

91

That night, I couldn't fall asleep. I kept thinking about what Mrs. Schimer had said about Naomi's grandfather. Naomi said that he had left Hungary seven years before the Germans invaded. Then how could he have been the last relative Mrs. Schimer ever saw? And I didn't get to ask her about Austria.

The next morning I told Naomi I *had* to speak to her during lunch. When I asked her my first question, she just shrugged.

"She was a little child." Naomi began twisting her long, blonde hair around her index finger. "She doesn't remember everything like a computer."

"Why does she have an Austrian accent?"

"Austria, Hungary, the borders were always changing. You know that from World History class."

"I guess so," I conceded, skeptically. "I still think it's strange, though."

"Do you want to come over later and we can ask her about it?"

"Sure."

"Come at four. I need to buy some shoes right after school, but I should be home by then."

I shook my head. "I have a piano lesson at four."

"Okay," Naomi hesitated. Her next words showed that she wanted to try and accommodate me. "Let's go right after school. I'll get my shoes later."

When we got to Naomi's house, no one was home except for her cousin, and she was on the phone talking in German. Once she heard us in the

house, she lowered her voice and cut the conversation short, but I had heard enough to make it hard to smile at her.

"Can we ask you some more questions, Magda?" Naomi asked.

Mrs. Schimer shook her head and seemed really agitated. "I'm on my way out. Maybe tomorrow." She practically ran out the door, if you can imagine an old woman in heels running.

"Sorry," Naomi said as the door was closing. "Do you want to come with me to get shoes?"

I ignored the invitation and glared at her.

"I thought your cousin was from Hungary?"

"Yes?" Naomi was surprised at my tone of voice.

"Why was she speaking German on the phone?"

Naomi looked at me as if I was nuts. "Most people, except Americans, know several languages."

"I might be an American, but I know German. And I'd like to know what secret meeting your cousin is going to."

"What are you talking about?" Naomi asked, getting more upset by the minute. She didn't like the way I was attacking her cousin.

"That's what she was saying on the phone," I explained, upset myself at the way she was reacting. "A secret meeting. Near Hinkley. At the farmhouse – while his daughter is away because the daughter is

not sympathetic."

"Where's Hinkley? Whose daughter? What farmhouse?" Naomi had her mouth opened wide.

"Hinkley is a small farming community about 40 miles north of Greenville. Most of the people from there come here to do their shopping. What does your cousin need to go there for? I don't know, but something is strange about Mrs. Schimer.

"And anyway, how do you really know she's your cousin? Your grandfather never saw her. Maybe she's just pretending to be your cousin."

"Why would she do that?" Naomi was staring at me as if I had gone absolutely crazy, so I took a deep breath and told her the rest of the conversation I had heard.

"Your 'cousin' said that she told them, whoever 'them' is, that everyone would be drinking so much they wouldn't notice anything suspicious."

Naomi began playing with her long hair, a sure sign that she was nervous.

"Where would there be so much drinking?" she asked. "The Jewish New Year's Eve is long past."

"But Purim isn't!" I retorted.

Naomi's face blanched. "So?" she asked, beginning to see the light.

"So I think," I explained, "that someone wants to sabotage the Purim dinner at the synagogue. Someone who doesn't like Jews." I really felt terrible about what I had just said. I still liked Naomi's cousin.

"But Magda is Jewish!" Naomi shouted, still

confused.

"How do you know?" I asked.

"All right," Naomi said decid-  edly. "Let's go into her room. She has a box with all her important papers in it. I bet she has her birth certificate in it, too."

With my heart pounding, I followed Naomi down the hall. She opened her cousin's bottom bureau drawer and pulled out a wooden box. On the top was her Israeli passport, then her marriage certificate, next her birth certificate, and finally some pictures. Her birth certificate had the name Marcus on it, and in one of the group pictures Naomi identified her grandfather. I felt like an idiot, until Naomi's sweater got caught on a hinge of the box and she discovered it had a false bottom. Opening it, she gave a gasp. Looking over her shoulder I saw a German passport. With shaking fingers, Naomi handed it to me and I opened it to see Mrs. Schimer's picture smiling at me. Underneath was written the name, Margot Schmidt.

I looked at Naomi and she looked at me.

All of a sudden, I was scared silly. What did I really know about Naomi's family? Maybe the whole lot of them were a group of ex-Nazis.

"What does this say?" Naomi handed me a note written in German.

"It says, *Hans Richter, 1224 W. Cable Road, Thursday, four p.m.* I bet that's the address and time of the meeting."

95

Before she could answer, we heard the unmistakable sound of high heels on the front walk. I froze, but Naomi didn't. Frantically, she stuffed all the paper back into the box and threw it back into the bottom bureau drawer. We were just a few inches from Magda's bedroom door when we heard the front door open and her heels clicking down the hall. Naomi grabbed my hand and we went flying under her cousin's double bed.

As we lay under the bed, holding our breath and trying not to make a sound, I felt Naomi's pulse racing. I wondered what my pulse rate was, and prayed silently that Naomi had returned the box just the way it was. There was a small space between the bedspread and the floor. I was able to watch Mrs. Schimer's heels as they came into the room and made their way to her closet, not the bureau. They stopped about six inches from the bed and then, to our relief, we saw them walk out of the room. We heard the *click, click,* as they went back down the hall and out of the house.

Naomi's next words totally allayed my suspicions of her.

"I think we should go to Hinkley and find this place. I bet there's a perfectly logical explanation for all of this. And if not, we'll go to the police."

"Okay," I answered hesitantly. "But how are we going to get to Hinkley?"

Naomi smiled proudly. "I've *almost* got my learner's permit. But don't worry, my mother took me out to the parking lot in the mall last week and let

me drive. She says that I'm a natural. I'll get a phone book to put under me so I look taller. Let's go."

In my saner moments, I might have thought twice about this adventure. But I was all excited with the prospect of catching a real Nazi.

Until we hit the highway, Naomi drove slowly and carefully. I was just feeling a little more secure about her abilities, when we entered the entrance ramp to route 24. Then, without warning, Naomi floored the gas pedal. We took off going eighty-five.

"Slow down!" I screamed. "Do you want the police to stop us?"

She slowed down to a respectable seventy and we were in Hinkley in no time. Just because we had an address, though, didn't mean we could find Cable Road easily. And we couldn't ask directions. But luck was with us. Literally two minutes after we arrived in town, we spotted Mrs. Schimer getting into a black car.

"I'm going to follow them as closely as possible," Naomi declared. I just held my breath.

We went about six blocks east, out of town, and then turned uphill onto a dirt road. After another five minutes, Naomi stopped the car. From behind the tree where we were parked, we could see Mrs. Schimer and a man going into a farmhouse across the road. There were several cars parked in the

driveway, but nothing looked unusual.

"I'll sneak over there," Naomi whispered.

"I'm coming with you," I volunteered.

I must have been brain dead. Every cop show has one cop covering the other. I should have stayed in the car, with the car phone, and watched Naomi. But I didn't.

We inched our way slowly across the yard moving from one tree to the next. Everyone was inside when we made it to the front porch. There was a big picture window, with enough room for us to sit underneath it. We didn't try to see inside – that would have been foolish – but we could hear perfectly.

"Now you, Tom," barked a deep male voice. "You need to be at the Jew church at seven. Sam will drop you off and drive around the block, while you place the bomb and – "

Just then, a German shepherd came bounding up the porch steps, barking his head off. We should have known a group of Nazis would have a guard dog. Before we could even think of running, the dog had me pinned to the floor of the porch, its front paws on my chest. Everyone came running out. An old man, a giant who must have been almost seven feet tall, was the first to reach us. Mrs. Schimer was in the back of the crowd and, when she saw us, she turned as white as a ghost.

With a blood-curdling "Ach! Juden!" the old man lunged at Naomi who was still standing upright. "What are you doing on my land?" he shouted, speaking an almost flawless English.

98

"We're lost," Naomi an-swered. She didn't miss a beat. Despite my fear, I looked up at her in admiration. "We wanted to ask directions."

"I'll give you directions to hell!" the man screamed. His face was wrinkled and he looked about ninety. But his arms were thick and muscular. He raised his hands, as if to choke Naomi, and muttered a command to the dog. It growled at me, showing its teeth.

Suddenly, we heard Mrs. Schimer's soft voice take command. "Lock them in the barn. We'll deal with them later. We must finish our plans before your daughter comes."

The giant mumbled a few words to the dog, and it released me. Instead of choking Naomi, he grabbed her with one hand and me with the other. With long strides, he pulled us to the barn where he swore at us and locked us in with a padlock. The smell of hay and manure surrounded us. A mare in her stall turned her head to look at us, and then returned to her oats. No other living creature was in sight, except for a mouse that scurried across the floor.

Naomi was silent. I couldn't tell if she was in shock or just taking the whole situation calmly. Once again, I was full of dread. Maybe Naomi had led me into a trap. Since I suspected her cousin, perhaps she wanted to get rid of me. Oh, why had I trusted her?

Would I ever see my home again? What would my mom think when I didn't come home? Why hadn't I told her where I was going?

All of a sudden, a ray of hope hit me. I looked at my watch. It was after four. Maybe my piano teacher had already called home to find out where I was. Maybe my mother had already called the police.

The sound of a sob shook me out of my thoughts. I glanced over at Naomi. Her face was soaking wet and she was wiping at it with the palms of her hands. Either she was a really good actress or she was as frightened as I was.

"Are you scared?" I asked, sympathetically.

Naomi nodded. "We were so stupid. We should have told someone where we were going."

There was nothing I could say to that. I agreed with her one hundred percent. "Let's look around the barn. Maybe there's a loose plank or something," I suggested.

We divided the barn in half and made our way slowly around the walls. That building was built better than some of the houses in Greenville. Nothing seemed loose until I reached the wall near the door. I pulled, and a bottom plank came free in my hands. Open mouthed, I stared at a brown manila packet.

"Naomi," I whispered.

She came quickly to my side. "Open it," she commanded.

Inside were some yellowed, official looking papers. The top one had a swastika on it.

"Can you read it?"

I nodded my head. "It's a letter of praise from Hitler." My hands shook, and so did my voice. "Put it back. I don't want to see anymore."

Naomi did as I asked and re-fastened the plank. We sat down with our backs against the wall and glumly contemplated our chance of getting out of the barn alive. It seemed as if we sat in silence, forever. Finally, Naomi broke the silence.

"You were probably really mad when the history teacher made us partners for the project."

"Umm." I didn't want to admit anything.

"You tried to be really nice and friendly when I first came, and I was a big snob."

"Umm," I repeated.

"I was really mad at the world when we came to Greenville. We were supposed to be going back to Israel, but instead we came here. By the time I was ready to be friends, everyone was disgusted with me. I acted like I didn't care, but I did. I'm sorry."

"It's okay. I should have given you another chance," I mumbled. "I tend to be really judgmental at times. Not that it really matters now. But – " I hesitated for a second. "If we survive this, I'll be happy to be your friend."

"Thanks," she smiled. Her face clouded and she gave a deep sigh. "We should have told someone where we were going," she repeated. "When I saw

101

that passport, I thought about my *savta*. I was so angry, I didn't think."

"What about your savta?" I asked.

"My mother's mother," Naomi explained. "She was in Auschwitz and lost all her family there. Every time I see the number the Nazis tattooed on her arm, I want to cry."

Now it was my turn to sigh. "I should have stopped to think, too. It's just that I was reading this book about a Nazi who pretended to be Jewish, and hid himself in a Jewish community to escape justice. All I could think was that we had to catch your cousin."

"I don't think she's my cousin," Naomi said, remorsefully.

Just then the door to the barn opened and we grabbed each other. I screwed my eyes shut and clamped my teeth tightly together so I wouldn't scream.

"Follow me, quickly!" I heard a women's voice say. I looked up to see Mrs. Schimer glaring at us. "You have almost spoiled all our work."

Taking us by the hand, she marched us to a corner of the barn. Kicking aside the hay, she revealed a trapdoor too.

"There's a tunnel under here that leads out behind the barn." She spoke urgently as she pulled the door open. "Get out of here as fast as you can."

We looked at her, immobilized with fear. Hastily, she pulled up one of the long sleeves of her dress. "Do you think I'm a Nazi?" she hissed, ripping

away a large band-aid she had on her forearm. "Nazis don't have this." She stuck her tattooed arm in our faces and gave us a push towards the trap door. "If they find out I helped you, they will kill me," she called after us. "If they ever see you again, they'll kill you too. Don't tell anyone anything about this. Do you understand?"

We didn't take time to answer. We scurried out the tunnel as if our lives depended on it, which they did. We were breathless when we emerged outside. Praying that no one would see us, we tiptoed back to the car. Fortunately, it was hidden behind a tree and on an incline, so we were able to coast backwards down the dirt road. We didn't turn the motor on until we were sure those in the house wouldn't be able to hear us. Then Naomi started the car, put it into gear, and raced off. Eighty-five seemed slow compared to what she was doing now.

"Wait a minute," I yelled, as we turned onto the highway.

"What's the matter?" Naomi screeched. "Are we being followed?"

"No," I shook my head. "But we can't just leave like this. They're planning to blow up the synagogue."

Naomi slammed on the brakes. "We've got to call the police."

"Okay," I nodded slowly.

Naomi's hand went to the car phone. We

looked at each other, remembering Mrs. Schimer's words, *Don't tell anyone anything about this!*

"Go ahead," I prompted. "We'd have to be crazy not to call the police after everything that's happened."

Naomi pressed 911 and handed me the phone. Taking a deep breath, I tried to explain as quickly as I could what was happening.

"Okay, miss," the dispatcher said in a bored voice. "But, you know it's against the law to call the police unless there really *is* an emergency, don't you?"

Hearing the response, Naomi grabbed the receiver. "This *is* an emergency! Lives are in danger! You've got to hurry!"

"Yes, miss," the dispatcher said, carefully taking our names, addresses, and all the particulars we could give him. "You girls go home and wait for someone to come by. I'll have a patrol car check the synagogue as soon as one becomes available," he concluded, hanging up.

"Oh, boy," I fumed. "I don't think he really believes us."

"By the time he sends the patrol car, there won't be any synagogue to check out."

Naomi and I looked at each other again. For having just become friends, it was amazing how much we could communicate without words. Carefully, Naomi turned around and we headed back to the farmhouse.

"If nothing else, we can stand watch," Naomi

said.

I nodded. "If anyone leaves, we'll follow them."

"Do you think that tattoo was real?" I asked, as we neared the place.

"I don't know," Naomi answered, concentrating on hiding the car behind a tree.

It was twilight and hard to see, but we could make out a group of five people standing in the farmyard near the barn. All of a sudden, we heard awful bellowing from the giant, and he was shouting in German.

"What is he saying?" Naomi asked.

"You let them loose, didn't you! *Didn't you*? You said you were making coffee for us but that took a long time. Now I know why!"

Then we heard a loud "smack" and a shriek that Naomi did not need for me to interpret.

"We've got to help her," Naomi declared.

"Okay." I followed her out of the car.

"What are we going to do about the dog?"

"Don't worry," I reassured her, as we crawled to the tunnel. "I heard the German commands that old man used. I can use them, too."

Once in the barn, we could hear everyone arguing in English. Apparently, only Mrs. Schimer and the old man knew German. They all seemed to be speaking at once, and it was hard to understand anything.

"We've got to distract them," Naomi said. Quickly, she outlined a plan and, for once, I was happy to take orders. I grabbed the pitchfork and she took the rake.

With our free hands, we snatched a roll of rope and hastily strung it across the barn door. We held it up about three inches from the floor. I banged on the barn door with the handle of the pitchfork while we both screamed at the top of our lungs, "Let us out of here!"

Boy, did they come running. All, except for Mrs. Schimer. Just as planned, the four that burst into the barn tripped over the rope. Before they even hit the ground, I had the pitchfork pointed at them, and Naomi was pointing the rake. I guess we didn't look as frightened as we felt because no one on the ground moved. It looked like our plan was going to work. In another second, we would slip out of the barn, close the padlock on them, grab Mrs. Schimer, and get out of there.

Just then, the dog came running in, barking his head off. I took a deep breath and gave the German command to calm it. But the dog didn't calm down. I guess seeing the old man on the ground confused it. It went straight to the old man, who was lying dazed on the floor, and began growling and baring its teeth at me. But before it could lunge at me, Mrs. Schimer appeared. Her hair was disheveled and she had a red mark on her face. But what really stood out about her was the small gun she held in her hand.

"Don't move any of you," she warned, pointing

the gun at the big man. "The police are already here, but if I have to shoot someone, I will."

Just then, we heard police sirens. I guess they had believed us, or Mrs. Schimer has somehow found time to call them. I never really did find out.

It didn't take long for the policemen to handcuff the four Nazis and restrain the dog. It turned out that the police had been working with Mrs. Schimer all along, and with – get this – Naomi's father. He and Mrs. Schimer weren't cousins; that was just a cover so they could work together. Teaching at the university was another cover. Mr. Marcus was a Nazi hunter. They had been hunting the giant, old man for a long time. Not only was he a notorious Nazi who escaped after the war, but he had managed to organize a neo-Nazi cell right in Hinkley.

The plan, we later learned, had been to catch him and his friends in the act of planting the bomb at the synagogue. Naomi and I had kind of gotten in the way.

It was okay, though. The manila packet we had found held enough evidence in it to put them all away for a long time. Add to that the conversations Mrs. Schimer had taped on her hidden recorder, and it was probably safe to say we would never have to worry about those animals again.

The police department wanted to give us an

award for our help, but our parents were against it. They didn't want us to get rewarded for being stupid and putting our lives in danger – twice. Also, Naomi's parents were just happy the police didn't press charges against their daughter for driving without a license. Her parents told her not to worry about getting a license to drive. The next time she would get a chance to drive a car would be some time in the next millennium.

Oh well. The best reward Naomi and I got was that now we were friends, good friends. She could be just as bossy as me, but we were able to work well together. Of course, now that the Nazis were caught, she and her family are getting ready to go back to Israel.

My mother says that maybe, in the summer, we will all take a trip to Israel.

Naomi and I can hardly wait.

Meanwhile, Naomi told me about her rich uncle in Israel. No one is quite sure what he does, but he travels a lot. Her mother says he's not really an uncle, it's just that everyone calls him that.

Sounds fishy to me.

What do you think?

How We Buried Hitler

By Bracha Weisbarth

About Bracha Weisbarth...

B racha Weisbarth was born in the Ukraine. When the German army occupied the region where she lived, her parents escaped to the forest, joined a partisan unit and fought the enemy. After liberation, the family lived for a few years in a Displaced Person camp in Germany, a temporary station on the way to the Land of Israel. In 1948, the family reached Israel, where Bracha grew up. She incorporated many of her own experiences in this story.

Bracha lives with her husband in Morristown, New Jersey, and works as the Director of Library Services of the Waldor Memorial Library of the Jewish Education Association of MetroWest. She has four granddaughters to whom she loves to tell her stories.

HOW WE BURIED HITLER

Great! thought Bruria on the last evening of summer vacation. Tomorrow the new school year starts, and I'll be in sixth grade. I can't wait to see all my friends again. I even miss my teacher, Zmira. It's so wonderful that she's moving up with us.

Bruria liked this feeling of continuity, which was a rare experience in her eleven years.

It was the fall of 1949. The new State of Israel was one year old and everything in it was new. Her Hebrew name, Bruria, was new as well, and she really liked it. She liked her new home in Yad Eliyahu, the new suburb of Tel Aviv, where her family had moved in the middle of the previous school year. She liked her new school, which was small and contained an equal number of *sabras* – children born in the Land of Israel – and *olim* – immigrant children who came to the newly established State of Israel. She liked her new friends who lived so close. One of them was her very best girlfriend, Ilana. Most of all, Bruria liked her teacher, Zmira, who was so kind and understanding. It was Zmira who helped her to feel so welcome when she joined the fifth grade in the middle of the school year.

When they first arrived in Israel, Bruria and her family stayed briefly in an immigrant absorption center. Bruria then went to live with her aunt and uncle in the town of Petach Tikvah, where she was to attend school.

In this school, Bruria was the first new *olah* that the other students, all *sabras*, had ever met. It was a difficult and painful experience for her. It was made even more difficult by the fact that Bruria's Hebrew was poor, her clothes were of a different style than those worn by the rest of the children, and her hair was done up in an old, European style that no one in Israel wore anymore. She was altogether too different to be accepted by the other kids. To top it off, the teachers in this school made no effort to make her feel welcome or accepted in the class.

It was a very lonely time for Bruria. She missed her parents, who still lived in the absorption center, even though they came to visit her as often as they could. This was the first time she had even been separated from them. She also missed the one thing that could relieve her solitude – her stamp album. When she asked her parents about it, she was told that their baggage, which contained her album, was still in a warehouse. Some months passed in this way, filled with sadness and longing.

One day, Bruria returned from school to find her parents waiting for her with exciting news. "Very soon we're going to live together again in our own apartment," her mother announced, beaming with happiness. This good news forced Bruria out of her

doldrums, as she eagerly waited for the move to her new home.

Bruria's family was assigned an apartment in a place called Yad Eliyahu, which was home to many Jewish soldiers, veterans of the British army who had fought the Germans during World War II. The few existing streets were lined with drab-looking houses. These houses were small but comfortable, surrounded by little gardens.

The site of the new housing project, which was intended for new immigrants, was an abandoned orange grove, where dry and gnarled orange trees, some still displaying small white blossoms, stood in orderly rows. The smell of the flowering orange trees was overpowering. It was like the smell of spring, better than any perfume Bruria had ever smelled. Hedges of wild rambling roses divided the citrus plots. Banana trees grew in a separate plot. To Bruria, this place seemed like paradise.

The new apartment buildings were quite different from the private homes. They were big, ugly, square blocks of gray concrete. They were being built as fast as possible in order to house the large number of new olim arriving in Israel. The backyards of these buildings were littered with leftover building materials. A few orange trees fought for their lives, a battle that was soon to be lost.

Bruria and her family were assigned a small apartment on the first floor. They received four iron

cots, a table, and four chairs to furnish their new home. Although the apartment was small and its furnishings poor, it was all theirs, and they felt very lucky to have it. At last they had a home of their own!

The whole family was busy making plans for decorating their new home and making it more comfortable. They retrieved their baggage from the warehouse, and soon the new apartment was transformed.

Bruria's parents found good jobs and had high hopes for their new life. Bruria's brother, Benny, was serving in the army, in a nearby camp, and came home almost every weekend. He even had an Israeli girlfriend.

Best of all, Bruria finally had her stamp album back. She put it in a place of honor, on the small bookshelf in her room. Soon enough, she even started adding new stamps to her collection – stamps of the State of Israel.

Even before being settled in their new home, Bruria's mother walked with her to the local school, where she was registered for the fifth grade.

From her first day in the new class, Bruria knew that everything in this school was going to be a lot better. For one thing, many of her classmates were newcomers to Israel, just like herself. She was no longer different from them. She belonged. In fact, she spoke better Hebrew than most of them. Her new teacher, Zmira, made her feel welcome in her new class and assigned one of the girls, Ilana, to help Bruria with homework. In no time at all, Bruria and

Ilana became best friends. When Zmira found out that Bruria had a lovely voice, she asked her to join the school choir.

Life in her new home and in the new school was just wonderful. It was great to feel welcome. How very lucky they were to be alive and in Israel, Bruria reflected.

When the Germans occupied the region of the Ukraine where they had lived before the war, Bruria's parents had fled to the forest and hid. Eventually, they joined the Partisans who fought the German soldiers. They lived in the forest until the end of the war. This was how the four of them survived. They were the only survivors of their entire extended family. They later learned that the Nazis had murdered all the other members of the family.

When the war ended, Bruria's parents felt that they could no longer stay in the Ukraine. They decided to leave Europe forever, and seek a new home in the Land of Israel. Even though Bruria had no real idea where or what the "Land of Israel" was, it seemed like a good plan to her. She was told that The Land of Israel was the "Promised Land," a place where all Jews could live in peace.

Long years of wandering from country to country ensued. For the next three years, nothing in Bruria's life was permanent. They never settled down in one place; they were always ready to pack their bags and continue on their journey to their final

destination. Eventually, the family arrived in West Germany, which at that time was occupied by the American Army.

For the next two years, they lived in a Displaced Person camp together with many other Jews from all over Europe who had survived the Holocaust. During their stay in the camp, Bruria, who was still called Bronia, attended a Hebrew school where she was taught to read and write Hebrew.

On her ninth birthday, her family gave her a gift, which became her most treasured possession – a large, beautifully bound stamp album. Her father bought the album from a German merchant, and it contained a valuable collection of German stamps. At first, Bruria was uneasy about the collection. Most of the stamps were from the Nazi era and carried the picture of Hitler – the accursed murderer of the Jewish people. Just looking at his face made Bruria sick with hatred. She wanted to get rid of these stamps – to burn them.

When Bruria told her father how she felt, he hugged her and said, "I know how you feel, Bronyale. I, too, find it hard to look at the hated face of Hitler. Try to overcome your uneasiness concerning these stamps. Try to think of this album as a very special symbol – a symbol of endurance and survival. Hitler, the vile murderer, is dead and buried, while we, his victims, are alive. Now this small Jewish girl can look at these stamps and triumph in knowing that she survived. She can add many more stamps to the

album, stamps that depict good things, from good places. One day, my darling daughter, you will able to add to your album stamps from the State of Israel. At that time, you will know that we have won."

Bruria found comfort in her father's words. From that time onwards, she started collecting stamps in earnest. She told everyone in the camp about her stamp collection, and soon her Jewish neighbors gave her their stamps. She received American stamps from the American soldiers who lived nearby. Every so often, her father and brother bought her little packets of stamps at the local stamp stores and gave them to her. As her collection grew, she spent many hours with the stamps, organizing them in geographical order, looking at their colorful pictures, and loving every minute of it. The stamp album was her prized possession. It was her best friend.

When the State of Israel was declared on May 15, 1948, the camp residents celebrated this momentous occasion. They knew that now they would be able to go to Israel, their homeland, which had opened its gates to receive all the survivors of the Holocaust. It was a time of rejoicing, and a time for packing their bags once again, in preparation for the journey to the Land of Israel.

Bruria wanted to take her album with her in her small traveling bag, but her parents explained to her that they had to travel light because there was

very little room on the ship taking them to Israel. The album had to be packed with the rest of their belongings, which would be sent to Israel, later, on a larger ship. She begged and pleaded to take the album with her, but she knew that her parents were right. Finally, with a heavy heart, she gave her album to be packed with the rest of their belongings, not sure if or when she would ever see it again.

Now, settled in her new home, Bruria had her cherished album. She also found a real friend in Ilana, with whom she spent a lot of time during the long, hot summer days. Ilana loved to look at the stamps in the album and hear the stories Bruria told her about some of the colorful ones from far away places. She urged Bruria to show the album to the rest of their classmates.

Ilana lived in one of the cozy, small houses down the road. Her father had served in the British army during World War II, and now he worked as a truck driver. Her mother, a nurse, worked in the local health clinic and was expecting another child. They had a dog, named Gibor, who seemed to like everybody.

Ilana's brown eyes held a mischievous twinkle that belied her quiet and ladylike looks. Her long brown hair was combed into two long braids that continuously danced with every movement of her head, as though they had a life of their own. She was

always ready to try new things, to find adventure where there was none. She was quite a daredevil and could run faster than any other girl in their class. Bruria would have gladly exchanged her brown curls for Ilana's long braids; while Ilana  kept wishing she had Bruria's curls on her head instead of the "long ropes" – as she called her braids.

When the summer vacation started, the two girls spent many hours exploring their surroundings, ranging far and wide in the abandoned citrus grove, trying to keep as far away as possible from the noisy construction sites.

One lucky day they found an old abandoned shack, hidden by a hedge of rambling roses. It was probably the hut where the grove workers had rested during the heat of day. The two friends decided not to tell anyone about this shack, and to turn it into their very own clubhouse. They furnished it with two old crates which they found near one of the houses, and decorated it with pictures that they cut out from old magazines, as well as with their own paintings. A broken vase, filled with dried brambles arranged artistically by Ilana, stood in the corner.

Bruria and Ilana spent many happy hours in their clubhouse. They both enjoyed reading, and named their shack "The Library" because of all the books they kept there. One of their favorite books was "Emil and the Detectives" by Erich Kastner.

It was a wonderful summer, but as the

vacation drew to a close, Bruria waited eagerly for the start of the new school year.

On the first day of school, Bruria walked slowly into the dusty schoolyard, eager to meet her classmates and her teacher, Zmira. They gathered in the schoolyard for assembly, standing in two rows. After a few words of greeting from the principal, Mrs. Gold, they marched in an orderly fashion into their classroom.

Bruria and Ilana sat together. It was a small class, just 23 students. Most of the kids Bruria knew from fifth grade. She greeted her friends with a happy smile, waving to Yanek, who sat two rows behind her. She liked and respected him.

Yanek was an oleh, just like Bruria. He came from Poland. He was a year older than the rest of them and should have been in the seventh grade. But he was held back in the sixth grade because he had had very little chance to attend school regularly while wandering from place to place, on the way to Israel. He was strong, smart, and a good friend. Bruria enjoyed talking and playing with him during recess.

She smiled at Amos and her heart skipped a beat. He was tall and handsome, with blond unruly hair, a tanned face, and smiling blue eyes. He was the best looking boy in her class and one of the smartest as well. She had a bit of a crush on him and hoped that Amos also liked her.

Once, during the summer vacation, she met Amos by chance, while walking in the abandoned citrus grove. He told her that he too liked to wander

around in the grove. He explained that rainwater, which was collected during the winter rains, was used for irrigation of the grove. Then he invited her to go with him to see the water-well. It was a deep well, but it held no water this late in the  summer. When they reached the well, which was surrounded by a low stone wall, they threw a stone into it. They counted the seconds until they heard the sound of the stone hitting the bottom, trying to determine the well's depth.

"Not many people know about this well," Amos confided. "I heard that its location was kept secret because it served the Haganah as a secret hiding place for their weapons."

Like Ilana, Amos and his family lived in one of the small, neat houses. Amos' father fought with the British army during the war. He was severely injured during the fighting, which left him paralyzed and confined to a wheelchair. His mother was a teacher in one of the lower grades in their school.

Amos spent a lot of time with his father, listening to his stories about the war, and helping him when needed. He also helped to take care of his younger brother and sister.

Zmira welcomed all the students. Then, she introduced the new students: a boy named Nissim, from Yemen; Kobi from Rumania; and Chaim, a recent arrival from Bulgaria. Two new girls, who sat right behind Bruria's desk, Yvette and Miriam

(Mimi), were both from France.

Zmira asked for volunteers to help the new students, and to be their special friends. Bruria volunteered to help Mimi, who actually lived two houses away from her own apartment house.

The teacher spoke about plans for the coming year: "We have a lot of studying to do this year. I expect all of you to do your best for me. This year you will also be studying a new subject, English, with a new teacher, Mrs. Rubin. I am sure you will like her."

At the end of the lesson, as Zmira was about to leave the classroom, Bruria approached her and asked for permission to bring her stamp album to show the class. Ilana, who stood next to her, burst out saying, "Please, please say yes. It is such a beautiful album."

The teacher smiled at Ilana's enthusiasm.

"It's a good idea, Bruria. In fact, I think that we should designate an hour each Friday for a 'Show and Tell' session, so that each one of the students will have a chance to tell something about themselves, or show us something interesting. You, Bruria, will be the first one. But let's just wait until after Rosh Hashanah to start this program."

Bruria was delighted with this decision, and waited eagerly for the first Friday after Rosh Hashanah to arrive, when she would show her album to her classmates.

When the appointed day arrived, Bruria's mother saw her putting the stamp album into her schoolbag.

"Why are you taking your album to school?" she asked.

"Ima, I promised Zmira to show my album to my class today. She thought that it would be a great idea. She said that each Friday, one of us is to bring something interesting to show to the class. I volunteered to be the first. Isn't it wonderful? I'm sure that the kids will love my album," Bruria said.

"I don't think that it's such a good idea," her mother said, worried. "Your collection is very valuable. I think that it would be better not to take it to school. Something might happen to it."

"Oh, Ima, don't worry, nothing will happen. I'll watch my album all the time – *trust me*," Bruria answered, and put the heavy bag on her shoulder. "Shalom Ima, I have to go now. I'm meeting Mimi to walk with her to school." Before her mother could say another word, she ran out of the apartment.

At school, the morning proceeded as usual. During the second period, Zmira turned to the class and said, "Well, students, today we are having the first 'Show and Tell' session. Bruria volunteered to show us her stamp album. She started to collect stamps while she was still in Germany. She has many interesting stamps and an interesting story to tell. Come up, Bruria, and show us your album."

Bruria stood in front of the class. She was not used to talking before an audience and felt a little shy. She held up the album and started speaking,

123

haltingly at first, but with more and more confidence as she saw her classmates become more and more interested in what she was saying. Bruria recounted how her father had given her this album. She pointed out how stamp collecting was such an interesting hobby because it introduced you to beautiful places all over the world. Then she walked from desk to desk, opening the album, to show some of the more exotic and valuable stamps in her collection.

"Hey, wait a minute, why do you have so many stamps of Hitler?" Dudik exclaimed, jumping up from his chair. "You should get rid of all those ugly stamps that show his ugly face. I really can't believe you kept them!"

A debate quickly broke out. Some students supporting Dudik, while others defended Bruria. Zmira quickly intervened.

"Calm down, class, calm down! This is not a marketplace. Let Bruria explain her reasons for keeping the Hitler stamps in her collection."

But before Bruria could open her mouth, there was a knock on the door. The principal, Mrs. Gold, walked into the classroom accompanied by an elderly man.

"Shalom, sixth grade," Mrs. Gold said. "I have a special visitor with me. This is Mr. Levine. He lives in one of the new houses right here in Yad Eliyahu. Just like many in this class, he is a new oleh who came just a short time ago from Germany. Mr. Levine is trying to find any relatives who might have survived the Holocaust. Please listen to him, and maybe you

can help him."

The visitor looked at the  children with a penetrating gaze. He was a man of medium build, bald, with a large prominent nose, and a wrinkled face. He wore dark-framed glasses. Under his heavy eyebrows, his brown eyes shifted from face to face, like two scurrying mice.

Mr. Levine spoke with a heavy German accent. "Good morning, my dear children. I am from Stuttgart, Germany, and now I live and work here. I am a civil engineer and an amateur archaeologist. I am looking for my cousins. I heard that they had survived Dachau and immigrated to Israel after the war. Their last names are Levine, Greenbaum, and Mayer. They all lived in Stuttgart before the war and owned stores there."

Looking directly at Bruria, who still stood in the front of the room holding her open stamp album, Mr. Levine continued.

"My cousin, Heinrich Levine, had a large bookstore in Stuttgart where he sold stamps and coins. He was an avid stamp collector. I, too, collected stamps, but the Nazis took them away from me. Now, I am just trying to collect my cousins." He emitted a short laugh, pleased with his sense of humor. "Do you know anyone named Levine, Greenbaum, or Mayer? If you know anyone by these names, please raise your hand."

The room was quiet. No one raised their hand.

125

After a moment, Mrs. Gold thanked the class and left, with Mr. Levine in tow.

Bruria was very glad to see them go. Mr. Levine made her feel uneasy, despite the fact that he was a fellow stamp collector. Something about the way he looked at her stamp album seemed quite sinister.

When they left, Bruria turned back to the class and, trying to keep her voice from trembling, she repeated what her father had told her about the importance of saving the stamps in her album. She concluded by saying, "Hitler is dead and we are alive. We survived him and we triumphed over his evil deeds. We can never let the world forget what a terrible man he was. I want my album to help the world remember the horrible times that just happened, as well as the wonderful times that are happening now. Look," she added, holding up a page of stamps, "my album already contains stamps from our own State of Israel."

The class remained quiet. Her words had obviously affected them all, even Dudik.

"Well said," their teacher commented, patting Bruria on her shoulder. "Thank you, Bruria, for showing us your collection."

The bell rang. It was time for gym class. The students rushed out of the class because they had to change their clothes. Bruria carefully put the album in her schoolbag and followed her classmates. When the gym class ended, Bruria did not bother to change. After all, gym was the last class of the day and she was in a hurry. She had to go home to finish her chores in

preparation for Shabbat.

Bruria, Mimi, and Ilana walked together, chatting about the events of the day. Amos, who usually walked home with them, must have been in a hurry that day. He was way ahead of them, walking  as fast as he could, almost running towards his house.

When Bruria arrived home, she started straightening up the apartment. She wanted to be finished before her mother arrived. This was her way of helping her mother, who worked full time. When, at last, she completed all her chores, she sat down with her school bag on her lap. The discussion in the class still bothered her, but she knew her father was right. People had to know that such evil existed in the world so that they would be on guard against it occurring again. She opened her school bag, reached in, and –

The album was gone!

Bruria emptied her school bag and searched through the house. Perhaps she had dropped it somewhere. But where? Then it came to her. Gym. She must have dropped it in the locker room as she was changing.

With tears in her eyes, Bruria ran back to school. But by the time she got to school, the school was locked. She hurried back home.

Inside her apartment, she sprawled down on her bed, trying to catch her breath after her mad dash

127

to and from school. Her thoughts were running in circles. "It must either be in gym or in my desk at school," she said to herself. "Either way, there's nothing I can do until Sunday, when school opens."

Bruria decided not to tell her mother about the missing album. She promised herself that on Sunday she would go to school very early, retrieve her album, and only then would she tell her mother what had happened.

To Bruria, the hours of that Shabbat day seemed to crawl. Finally, on Sunday morning, she ran to school. She rushed to her locker in the gym, but the album was not there. She charged up the steps towards her class, banged opened the door, and stood in front of her desk. Slowly, she opened the lid with trembling hands – the album was not there!

The reality of seeing the empty desk hit her all at once. She finally had to accept the fact that her album was really missing. Bruria sank into her chair, tears streaming down her cheeks.

Who would do such a thing? Who took my album? she kept thinking. She felt guilty for not listening to her mother and for not telling her parents that the album was missing. But above all, she felt angry. How could someone take something which did not belong to them? Taking the album without permission was stealing. She had to find the album and expose the thief. She had to punish him or her, shame whoever did it in front of the whole school.

By the time her classmates started arriving in class, Bruria calmed down a little. She walked out of

the classroom and stood by the door. She decided to wait for Zmira outside the classroom, tell her about the missing album, and ask for her help.

When Ilana came to class, Bruria immediately confided in her.

"Wait a minute, I think I have a better idea," Ilana said, jumping up and down with excitement. "Why don't the two of us form a detective team, just like the young detectives in the book we read this summer. Together, we'll find the thief who stole your album and get it back." She stopped talking and pulled thoughtfully on one of her braids. "Maybe it would be even better if we asked some boys to join our team. Let's ask Amos and Yanek to join us. The four of us will solve this crime."

Bruria agreed, but first she wanted their teacher to talk to the class. Maybe she could appeal to the thief's better side.

Just then, their teacher arrived. Bruria told her about the missing album and asked for her help. Zmira looked very concerned. She stroked Bruria's brown curls, looked into her tear-filled eyes, and said, "Don't worry Bruria, I'll talk to the class. I can assure you that you will get your album back. Now take your seats."

Zmira walked into the classroom, put down her bag, and turned to face the class. She stood there for a long minute, examining each and every one of her student's faces. Then, in a serious tone of voice,

she said, "A very bad thing happened on Friday. Bruria's stamp album disappeared from her bag. Look at her, she is very upset, and so am I. Remember what we learned in the Torah about the Ten Commandments? The eighth commandment says, 'Thou shalt not steal.' I am afraid that someone in this classroom broke this commandment. I hate to think that someone in this room took the album, but if it's true, I ask that the person who took the album return it to Bruria right away. I don't want to know who did it. I promise you that if the album is returned by tomorrow, I will drop the matter altogether. It will be the end of the story.

"I hope that you all remember that right now we are in the period between Rosh Hashanah and Yom Kippur. The period known as the *Ten Days of Atonement.* Any person who committed a sin, but who atones for it during these ten days, is forgiven. As we prepare for Yom Kippur, we must remember that it's not too late to find forgiveness."

A hush fell over the students when Zmira finished talking. Bruria observed the reactions on her classmates' faces, but she did not see anyone showing guilt or hanging their head in shame. She was disappointed, expecting instant results from the teacher's words.

"Now class," Zmira continued, "let's proceed with our lesson. Please take out your history books," she said.

During recess, the whole sixth grade gathered around Bruria, voicing their concern and anger;

offering their support. Ilana took  Amos and Yanek aside and talked to them in private. Afterwards, she told Bruria, "Let's meet after school at our clubhouse. I asked Amos and Yanek to join us there at four o'clock."

That afternoon, the four friends met at the clubhouse. Bruria told the boys about Ilana's idea, that they act as detectives in order to find her missing album. Yanek was very excited at the prospect of playing detective. To him, the whole thing was an exciting game, a real-life adventure. Bruria on the other hand, was subdued, still feeling a keen disappointment that their teacher's words had not convinced whoever took her album to return it. Amos, too, was quiet and pensive, as though he had other things on his mind.

Ilana came late, bursting into the clubhouse like a canon ball. "I saw your stamps! I saw your stamps!" she shouted. "Right in the window of a shop on Allenby Street. Let's go, I'll show you!" She ran out and they followed her, running, to the bus stop, without asking any questions.

The No. 9 bus took them to the main street of Tel Aviv. They got off the bus and followed Ilana to a store selling old coins and stamps. In the center of the window, stamps featuring the face of Hitler were displayed. The group looked at Bruria. She stared at the stamps, trying to remember if they were identical to hers.

131

"I'm not really sure those are my stamps," she admitted.

"Well, go into the store and ask the owner," Yanek commanded.

Bruria walked into the store while her friends waited outside. She spoke briefly with the owner, then joined her friends.

"I-I don't know. I'm not sure," she stammered.

"What did the store owner say? Where did he get those stamps?" asked Ilana.

"He said that he bought them on Friday from a man who spoke with a German accent. He didn't see any album, just an envelope with those stamps," Bruria explained.

"What was the name of that German fellow who came to our class on Friday?" Yanek asked out loud.

"Mr. Levine," Amos said.

"Mr. Levine. That's right," agreed Yanek. "I bet he saw Bruria's album, waited for his chance, and then stole the album," Yanek declared triumphantly. "German accent, German stamps. These are no coincidences."

"Let's go back to the clubhouse and decide what to do," suggested Ilana. They all agreed.

When they returned to the clubhouse, Bruria spoke up at once.

"I think it was this man, Mr. Levine," she said. "What business did he have to come to our school? I know that if you are looking for surviving relatives, you write to a special government office and ask for

their help. We did this when we came to Israel." She took a deep breath and continued, "You heard him say that he collected stamps, too."

The clubhouse grew quiet; all four members were deep in thought.

"The question is, what do we do now?" Ilana said, voicing what each of them was thinking. "We don't have enough proof to go to the police, or even the principal."

"As I see it," Bruria said, "the first step must be to find out where Mr. Levine lives, and then try to discover where he hid the album. There were many more stamps in the album, some of them more valuable than the ones with Hitler's picture. I doubt if he will stop at just selling some of the stamps. He'll probably look for another store to sell the rest, so no one will be suspicious. We have to find the album before he sells all the stamps." She turned to Ilana and added, "Ilana, try to get his address from the school secretary. I'm sure that you can come up with some believable reason for needing his address."

Yanek looked at Ilana. "As long as you're doing the checking up on people, perhaps you might speak to Chaim, the custodian, and find out if he saw anyone suspicious entering our classroom while we were out. You never know, maybe one of the students came into the locker rooms. We can't afford to eliminate anyone as yet."

"I think that Bruria should ask Mrs. Gold to make an announcement during school assembly, about the missing album," Amos added.

They all decided to meet the next day and report their progress. Bruria prayed that her mother would not ask her about the album.

Monday was no different from Sunday; the album was still missing. Bruria, accompanied by her teacher Zmira, spoke with Mrs. Gold, who agreed to make an announcement about the missing album. A talk with Chaim, the custodian, did not bring any results. He was unaware of anyone going into their classroom, but he mentioned that he did see an unfamiliar man walking in the hallway.

The group met in the afternoon. Ilana produced a scrap of paper with Mr. Levine's address on it. "I told the school secretary that I needed his address to give to my father who knows a family named Levine. This happens to be the truth," she said with a mischievous smile.

"All right, it's time for action," Yanek said. "Let's go to his apartment and investigate. At this time of the day, he is probably still at work."

"I can't," burst out Ilana. "Today is my turn to walk our dog and there's no one else to do it."

"That's all right. Why don't you take Gibor and join us near Mr. Levine's house. You can stand guard while we investigate," Bruria said.

Ilana went home to fetch her dog, while the rest of the group walked toward Mr. Levine's place. It turned out that he lived on the ground floor of an

apartment building. Ilana went into the building and rang the bell. She rang it until she was sure no one was home.

"Okay," she told the others, "let's go inside."

The three of them climbed through an open window and found themselves inside Mr. Levine's living room.

"Let's try his bedroom door," Amos suggested.

They walked through a narrow hallway and came to the bedroom door. Amos tried to open it, but it was locked.

"Who locks their bedroom?" he said, surprised.

"No one," Ilana answered, "unless he has something to hide."

For a moment, it seemed that their investigation had come to an end. Then, Yanek had a brilliant idea.

"Hey guys, these houses were built so cheaply that the builder installed the same locks in many doors, especially on the inside doors. One of our neighbor's kids locked himself in the bathroom and someone was able to use our key to open the door. Let's see if this will work here. Bruria, give me your keys. Maybe we will be able to open this door."

First, Yanek tried opening the door with his key, but it didn't fit. When he tried Bruria's, there was an immediate *click*. The door opened.

"Hurry, hurry!" Yanek whispered. They

135

searched everywhere, but didn't find a thing. They locked the door on their way out of the bedroom and then checked the living room again. Nothing.

The album was not here; or else it was too well hidden. Suddenly, they heard barking.

"Ilana and Gibor are here," Bruria said. "Let's go."

Ilana and Gibor were in the backyard of the apartment house. Ilana was very excited.

"I saw Mr. Levine walking into the citrus grove," she said, pointing. "He was walking along the path, in the direction of the stand of banana trees, carrying a bundle and a shovel. Come on, let's run, or we might lose him," she urged. Gibor jumped up and down, expressing his joy at being invited to give chase.

Everyone started running in the direction that Ilana had pointed. They all knew exactly where the banana trees were located, in a plot separate from the rest of the grove, protected by a dense hedge of wild, climbing roses. A few minutes later they saw Mr. Levine walking sedately along the path, unaware anyone was following him. Suddenly, he turned off the path and disappeared among the banana plants. The group rushed forward.

"Shh...Shh? Keep quiet. Let's not scare him," whispered Bruria. Mr. Levine appeared once again, strolling among the plants, as though searching for something.

"Hide behind the hedge," Yanek whispered.

They ran forward and hid behind the dense

136

hedge of climbing roses, trying to see what Mr. Levine was doing. He took his bundle and laid it on the ground, moved away some fallen banana leaves with a shovel, knelt down and started digging, his back to the group.

"My album! He's burying my album! Let's go and get it," Bruria whispered in an excited voice.

Without thinking, they rushed towards the kneeling Mr. Levine, Gibor leading the way. When they reached their prey, they almost fell over him. Mr. Levine was so startled he fell back, revealing the bundle, which in their minds contained the album. Unfortunately, it was only a collection of tools and brushes spread out on a piece of tarpaulin.

"Shalom, dear children, what are you doing here?" Mr. Levine greeted them, as he lifted himself into a sitting position. "You certainly managed to scare an old man," he lightly scolded.

They stood next to him, like pillars of salt, unable to move, unable to answer his greeting. Gibor saved them from further embarrassment. He walked over to Mr. Levine, sniffed him, and then proceeded to lick his dirt-encrusted hands.

"Oh...Ah...Shalom...the dog, we were walking the dog," Amos answered for all of them.

Mr. Levine accepted this explanation. "Good doggie, nice doggie," he said, patting Gibor. "This is a nice dog. Dogs like me."

"Why are you digging here?" asked Yanek.

"Dear children," answered Mr. Levine, "I am an amateur archeologist. The Land of Israel is an archaeologist's dream. Dig anywhere and you are bound to find some shards, or broken pieces of ceramics, left by the people who lived here many centuries ago. I have already found a few interesting pieces. If you are interested, come and visit me, and I will show you my finds."

Bruria was very embarrassed, and looking at her friends she saw the same emotion mirrored on their faces. In a flash, they all realized that this was the wrong suspect.

"Help, help!" a tiny voice called out from the hedge. They turned around. Ilana! Where was Ilana? They ran to the other side of the rose hedge, and there she was, all tangled up among the rose thorns, unable to move. They burst out laughing, while Ilana smiled helplessly back at them.

"Get me out of here," she begged.

They tried to stop laughing long enough to free her from the thorns. Mr. Levine joined them, and finally Ilana was free. Her arms and legs were covered with many red scratches.

"My dear girl, you need to be seen by a doctor," said a very concerned Mr. Levine. "The rose thorns are very dusty after a long, dry summer. Your scratches might get infected. You will probably need a tetanus shot as well. Promise me you will see a doctor."

They were all touched by his concern.

"Don't worry, my mother is a nurse. She'll take

care of me," Ilana answered. Then they thanked Mr. Levine for his help.

"Gibor likes Mr. Levine," Ilana commented. "My dog has a good nose for judging people. He's never wrong. I think that Mr. Levine must be a fine person."

The group turned back, walking along the path in silence. From time to time, a giggle would escape from one or the other of them.

When they reached the clubhouse, Yanek summed up the situation, saying, "Mr. Levine is not our thief. I think that he is really very friendly, even if he sounds so...so funny. He is a little strange, but harmless. It seems the stamps we saw in the window must have belonged to someone else. Just a coincidence that they appeared in the store when Bruria lost her album. Now, how do we continue with the investigation? Can you think of any other suspects?"

"I have an idea," Ilana said. "We need to flush out the guilty person."

"That's a great idea, Ilana," Yanek agreed. "But how can we do it?"

"I suggest that we write notes to each one of our classmates and put those notes in their desks. Then, we should keep a very sharp lookout to identify anyone who acts guilty," Ilana said.

They all agreed that this was a good plan. It was decided that each one of them would write five notes

139

saying, *We know that you took the album! Return it to Bruria and all will be forgiven!* They would sign the note, *The Shadows.*

"Great name," Amos said, after Yanek came up with the title for their little band of detectives. "We'll stick to anyone who looks suspicious like their own shadow." Everyone laughed, excited by the prospect of actually catching the thief.

On Tuesday, the album was still missing. The four friends met early in the schoolyard, each with five handwritten notes. Bruria collected the notes and checked to see that they all had the same message on them. Then she walked into the classroom. The other three members of *The Shadows* followed her. She put a note into the desk of each one of her classmates, including her three friends. She didn't want anyone getting suspicious.

As her classmates entered the classroom and discovered the notes in their desks, *The Shadows* were ready. They observed the surprised reaction of their classmates and their indignation at being accused of stealing the album. Some tore up the note in anger; others showed it to their friends, as though unable to believe the message it contained.

Ruthie, one of the more sensitive girls in the class, burst out crying. "This is terrible, terrible. It's really cruel," she wailed.

Clearly, the team's ruse did not work. Not one of the students showed any guilt, embarrassment, or remorse. On the contrary, it was Bruria who felt remorse. She realized that the notes were indeed a

cruel trick, and that they hurt innocent people. Her precious album was not worth all this. She wanted to apologize to her class-mates, to ask for their forgiveness.

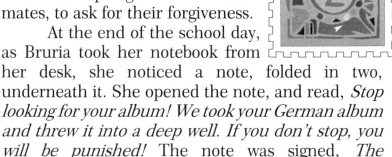

At the end of the school day, as Bruria took her notebook from her desk, she noticed a note, folded in two, underneath it. She opened the note, and read, *Stop looking for your album! We took your German album and threw it into a deep well. If you don't stop, you will be punished!* The note was signed, *The Organization of Jewish Avengers.*

The note was printed in large block letters. Under the signature was a drawing depicting a knife dripping blood, stuck through a swastika, the hated Nazi symbol. Something about the note looked familiar to Bruria, but she could not pinpoint it. She took the note and ran out to the schoolyard to find her friends.

"I have some important news, a new development," Bruria said in an excited voice. "Read this note. Read it and tell me what you think of it?"

"Another group? Like ours?" Yanek asked. "These people sound really mean. I think we have to be careful how we proceed."

"Wait a minute! The well! In the grove!" Bruria felt certain now. She knew where to find her album.

"Remember, Amos, you showed it to me. My album must be at the bottom of the well."

141

"That's crazy," Amos said. "Why would anyone want to throw your album into a well. The stamps are all enclosed in plastic. Throwing the album into water wouldn't destroy them at all."

"That's what I was thinking," Bruria said, excitedly. "All we need is a long, strong rope, and we'll be able to bring the album up."

"No, no!" Amos said, concerned that someone might get hurt. "The well is deep and too dangerous to climb down into. Even with a rope, it's easy to slip."

But *The Shadows* were too close now to give up because of a little danger. Yanek said that he knew where he could borrow a rope and told them to meet him at the clubhouse in an hour.

"Don't forget to bring along flashlights," Ilana advised.

They returned to the clubhouse, each with a flashlight. They waited tensely for Yanek to join them. When he showed up carrying a coiled rope and a flashlight, they walked toward the well. Amos led the way.

When they reached the well, Amos threw a stone into it. As he suspected, the well was dry. Even with the recent rains, whatever water that had collected in the well had dried. The foursome stood looking down into the deep, dark interior.

"I'll climb down into the well," Amos said in a firm voice. "Here, let's tie the rope to this tree stump; it looks strong enough to hold my weight. When I reach the bottom, I'll shout and turn my light towards you three. If I'm ready to come back up, I'll flash

twice. That's the sign to pull me up. And please, everyone pull together. I don't want to stay in the well forever. It looks like it may rain soon," he warned, looking up at the cloudless sky. The others realized he was joking, and smiled.

Bruria closed her eyes for a second. "Amos is so very brave. He's a real hero, and he is doing this dangerous thing for me," she thought.

Wordlessly, aware of the danger, they lowered Amos very slowly into the well. They waited breathlessly to hear the sound of his feet reaching the bottom. After what seemed like an hour, they saw his light shine upward. Then, long moments later, they saw the flashlight blink twice. Everyone grabbed the rope and started pulling. It wasn't an easy job, but finally Amos' hands appeared above the rim of the well. He pulled himself out, and lay panting at their feet.

"Boy, it really stinks down there," he said. "It's a good thing you helped pull me out. I doubt if I could have climbed up myself." Then, looking at Bruria, he continued, "Sorry, Bruria, your album was not there, and I didn't find any Haganah guns down there, either."

"Well, at least we know that note was just a hoax," a cheerful Ilana announced.

"This isn't the only well in Israel, you know," Amos told her. "But it's the last well I'm ever going down," he said, smiling.

143

When she returned home, Bruria went to her room, tired from the day's ordeal. She was fairly certain she would never see her treasured album again. It was very quiet in the apartment, when suddenly the doorbell rang. Bruria walked to the door, wondering whom it might be. When she opened the door, Amos stood in the hallway half turned away from the door, as though ready to run away. He looked nervous and pale.

"Shalom, Amos. What happened? Are you okay? Are you locked out?" Bruria had never seen Amos so nervous. "Don't just stand there, come in."

Amos stood speechless at the door.

Then, she saw a package in his hands, and an unbelievable thought flew through her mind.

A package...the size of her album.... Could it be? She felt a chill run down her spine.

"Here is your album, Bruria. Please forgive me. I didn't mean to steal it. I am so sorry." The words burst out of his mouth as he pushed the album into Bruria's hands. "I know you hate me, but you have to understand. When I saw the pictures of Hitler in your album, all those years of wandering, all the horror of what my family went through suddenly rushed over me again. I thought I would never have to think about the Nazi who shot my father and made him a cripple for life, or the murderer who shot little Moishele, my sister's son, just because he cried at the wrong time.

"When I saw those stamps, something clicked inside of me. I knew I had to take the stamps and

destroy them, erase them as you would an Amalekite, as you would anyone who builds his life upon the ashes of our people.

"So I took the album when you weren't looking, and brought it home. But by the time I got home, my anger had subsided. I realized that maybe you were right, maybe collecting Hitler stamps will remind us of all the countries who thought murdering Jews was okay. Maybe it was right to remind the world what monsters they could hold up as heroes. Before I knew it, I had decided to return your album. I was planning to tell you how I found it near the gym, where you must have dropped it. I figured I would be a big hero over the whole incident.

"Then I made the mistake of leaving the opened album on my bed. I went to the bathroom to wash up and while I was busy, my mother came into my room and saw the album. Suddenly, she screamed and I ran out of the bathroom thinking that something had happened to my father; his heart has been so weak lately. When my mother saw me, she started to shout at me. 'How could you collect such garbage?' she yelled. 'Don't you have any feelings for your father?' she screamed. I-I tried to explain, but before I could say a word she grabbed the stamps of Hitler and tore them to bits."

Amos took out an envelope with the torn stamps of Hitler and handed it to Bruria. He was sweating, even though a cool breeze entered the

145

apartment through the opened door.

"Bruria, I am so very, very sorry for the pain I caused you," Amos continued in a low, sad voice, "and for deceiving you. I did a terrible thing, taking your album without permission. I am so ashamed. I deserve the worst punishment you can think of. Please, please forgive me. Tomorrow I will confess my guilt in front of the whole class, and take my punishment. But first of all, I need to know that you can forgive me." Tears were running down his pale cheeks.

Bruria held her precious album. It was intact. Then a small envelope fell out and a pile of torn bits of paper, like colorful confetti, fluttered to the floor. It was all that was left of her Hitler stamps.

Anger flared up in her as she looked at Amos, and then at the torn stamps. But as she saw how wretched he felt, her anger began to dissipate. She realized that the album was not worth such suffering.

For a long time my album was my only friend, she thought, but now that I have so many real friends, I can let go of my album.

"I forgive you," she said aloud, in a determined voice. "This is the end of the story. Tomorrow I will tell Zmira that I found the album. I will say that my brother, Benny, borrowed it to show to a friend in the army. It's not right that Hitler, even his likeness on these stamps, should cause Jews such pain. But I have a good idea what we can do with these stamps," she announced.

She knelt down, collected the torn stamps,

and put them back into the  envelope. Then she went into the kitchen and took an old spoon from the drawer. Holding the small white envelope and the spoon, she lead Amos toward the orange tree growing in the back yard. She knelt beside the tree and handed the spoon to Amos.

"Here, Amos, in order to finally get rid of your memories of Hitler you must dig a hole in the ground," she commanded. Amos did as he was told. When the hole was deep enough, Bruria placed the envelope in the hole.

"Look, Amos, we're burying Hitler! We're burying hatred and anger. It is all in the past. Now is the time for a new beginning," she exclaimed, as she covered the stamps with the soil of Israel.

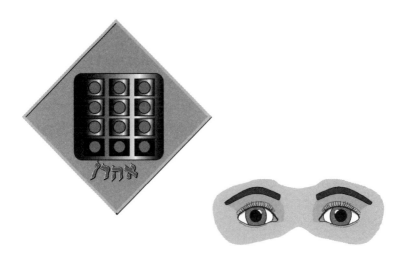

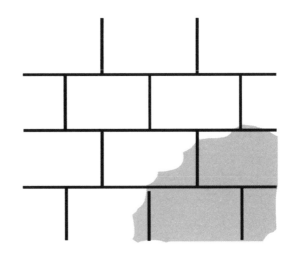

Speak No Evil

by Yaacov Peterseil

149

About Yaacov Peterseil...

Having nine children uniquely qualifies me to write a detective story.

Hardly a day goes by that I don't find myself interrogating at least one of my children for minor crimes and misdemeanors, like finishing my favorite ice cream and leaving the empty container in the freezer, for me to find. And there are secret plots galore, like when my daughter tried to cover up for the dog (a Giant Pyrenees Mountain Dog) when it ate most of my Shabbat suits – leaving me one trouser leg and a jacket pocket.

But I'm not complaining. I never run out of ideas for my books and stories, and I rarely have to make up anything. Most of the time what happens in my family *is* stranger than fiction.

And besides, not that many parents qualify to be a gumshoe.

SPEAK NO EVIL

H e moved quietly through the street, trying to keep close to the walls of the private homes. Suddenly, he stopped and looked at a corner of one of the houses. In the light of the street lamp, he could see the greenish tinge on the bricks.

He hoped he was not too late.

Without warning, he burst into the house. The smell of decaying flesh almost made him run out of the house. There, on the floor were two people, both alive. But the terrible look in their eyes, and the boils on their bodies, told a story he had seen too many times before.

"God protect them," he whispered, as he dialed for an ambulance.

It must have been past midnight when I snuck out of the house. It was pouring rain, and I ran the whole way to the hospital. I arrived there drenched. The hospital lights seemed so inviting compared to the cold rain that was falling on me.

I went in through the back entrance. The back entrance is an entrance most people don't know about. It's used for delivering medicines and things like that. No one ever watches the back entrance. I guess people just don't expect someone to sneak *into* a hospital. But, after all, it wasn't exactly visiting hours, so I figured that if the nurses on-call saw me,

they wouldn't think twice about kicking me out.

Assuta Hospital is eight stories high. It's also the tallest building in Mevasseret, a suburb of Jerusalem. Unlike most hospitals, the top two floors are research labs. You need special security clearance to get onto those floors. Even my dad, who is a terrific doctor, and well-known throughout the country, is never allowed up there. The other six floors have regular wards. That is, until about a month ago. Then floor six suddenly became restricted. I've tried to get in plenty of times, but the skull and crossbones sign on the elevator doors makes it clear that no one without special authorization can get in. The two guards at the elevators sort of add to the feeling that you just aren't wanted.

Once I entered the hospital, I knew exactly where I was going, and how to get there. I made my way through the deserted kitchen and reached the "Patients Only" elevator. I got in and pressed six. The elevator moved silently upward as my heart began to race. I quickly put on a patient robe that I had "borrowed" from the supply room. If someone stopped me, I was going to say that I was hungry and thought that the sixth floor was the cafeteria. It sounded reasonable to me. I hoped it would sound that way to anyone who caught me.

The "Patients Only" elevator on the sixth floor is around the corner from the regular elevators. Luckily, no one thought to guard the elevator so late at night. When I got out, I saw that the corridor was

empty.

I started walking towards my friend's room. Mr. Crown wasn't actually a friend, but during the time he had been here (he arrived about three months ago), we had become pretty close. Every day he sort of waited for me to come and cheer him up. The truth is, I looked forward to cheering him up. That is, until they suddenly put him – and the whole floor – under quarantine.

As I got close to his room, I could see that the door was slightly open, and I could hear Dr. Zabberwatz talking. I looked around. The guards were nowhere in sight, so I leaned my head against the door to listen.

"Just tell me," pleaded Mr. Crown. "Am I going to die?"

"Like I said, Mr. Crown," Dr. Z. answered, in his best *how-can-you-question-me-I'm-the-greatest* voice, "we're doing the best we can. I'm sure everything will turn out okay."

You may have guessed that I can't stand Dr. Zabberwatz. His deep voice sends chills down my spine. I heard Mr. Crown and Dr. Z. arguing for a while; Mr. Crown pleading for more information, and Dr. Zabberwatz insisting he really didn't know much more.

"I'll tell you more as soon as I know more," the doctor said in a final sounding tone, ending the conversation.

I hid behind the staircase door just as Dr. Z. came out of the room. I saw the doctor close the door and slide a latch. I had never seen any hospital room locked from the outside before.

As soon as Dr. Zabberwatz left, I approached the door. I put my hand on the latch, but stopped abruptly, remembering what Dad had told me earlier that day.

"I know, Nathan, that you like to visit me at the hospital. But I don't want you coming here anymore!"

"Why?" I had asked. Dad didn't know about my friendship with Mr. Crown.

"Nathan," Dad said, sounding so serious I got the shivers, "there are too many diseases in the hospital. Terrible diseases. I'm just afraid you might catch something."

I didn't have a doubt in my mind that something was fishy. After three years of spending my free afternoons following Dad around on his rounds, why would it suddenly be so risky now?

And then there was that phone call that I overheard. Dad was speaking to Dr. Zabberwatz, saying, "Anyone who has suffered from it has either died, or somehow disappeared."

I didn't know if it was drops of sweat or drops of rain that were trickling down my face, but I suddenly felt hot in my wet clothes. With two trembling hands, I opened the latch to Room 13 and walked inside. I stopped abruptly at the sight of what was lying in a bed across the room from me: a man,

154

about the age of thirty, with patches of snow-white skin on his face, head, and arms. Tufts of hair were missing from the white patches.

"What are you doing in here, kid?" asked Mr. Crown. "You know no one is allowed in here, especially since whatever-I-have started getting worse. You better go home. But I appreciate you coming, Nathan, I really do." His eyes looked so scared, I was almost tempted to run out of the room.

"I uh...," I mumbled. I felt like crying. The man looked awful. "I, uh, just wanted to find out how you're doing. What happened? Last week, you looked like you were getting better."

"That's the way it is with this fungus," Mr. Crown explained. "For a while it looks like it's getting better and then suddenly it flares up like sun spots. The doctors think I may have gotten something from the plants I deal with, something really rare. But I've been a gardener for years and I never handle foreign plants. I just don't get it."

He seemed so lost.

"What you have isn't so rare," I informed him.

"It is, considering I'm the only man that has it. That's what the doctor told me."

I stepped closer to Mr. Crown, bending so that I almost touched his ear. The white spots on his face looked like they were deeper than the rest of his skin. Talk about weird!

"All the rooms on six are occupied by patients

who have the same disease you do," I whispered. "I know, because there are guards on this floor and each room has the same sign you have on yours, 'Quarantine'. And each door has new latches on the outside, just like yours."

"Latches? You mean they lock me up in here?" Mr. Crown asked. His face had that strange *out-of-it* look, as if he had just been woken up from a deep sleep.

"Didn't you know?" I said.

Mr. Crown shook his head. "That explains why they won't let me have a phone or a television. They want to keep me isolated from everything. But why would they tell me I'm the only one with this disease?"

"I don't know. Maybe they're afraid you'll try to contact the other people with the disease." I swallowed hard. I just had a terrible thought. "Maybe you're so contagious that...."

"Oh, my God! What are you doing here?" Mr. Crown suddenly asked, reading my mind. He looked angry. I moved backwards, towards the door. If he really was as contagious as he looked, then I was in trouble. BIG trouble.

"I-I think I better go now, Mr. Crown," I hastily said, turning towards the door. "I just realized – "

The door to the room swung open, whacking me. I fell to the ground.

"Nathan!" Dr. Zabberwatz shouted, almost as startled as I was. He looked very big, towering above me.

Between my pain and my fear, I didn't know what to do. So, I did nothing.

Dr. Z. bent down and, not-so-gently, grabbed me by my ear. "You foolish boy! We're going to call your father right now and make sure you understand what you've gotten yourself into."

It wasn't that I was really scared of what my father might do. But I was terrified of Dr. Z. and what *he* might do to me. He was pulling my ear pretty hard and I thought I could see a scalpel sticking out of his hospital coat. I was sure he was getting ready to surgically separate me from my ear. I knew I had a second ear, but I had become really attached to this one.

So I kicked him in the shin, and pulled out of his grasp. Once free, I raced out of the room, down the stairs, out the hospital, and back into the rain. Actually, I didn't stop running until I got home.

At the door to my house, I took a breath, trying to calm myself down. Then, with trembling fingers, I unlocked the door.

The house was dark and quiet.

"Uh-oh," I mumbled to myself. I was leaving wet footprints everywhere. I grabbed a towel from the hallway closet, sat on my knees, and tried to wipe up the wet footprints. Then I took off my shoes and tip-toed towards my room. I had to get out of my dripping wet clothes. As I passed my parents' room, I was surprised to hear them talking quietly to each other.

157

I looked at the closed door to their room, straining my ears. No...no...they weren't talking. They were *arguing* about something. I turned and tiptoed to my room.

About three feet from my door, a terrible thing happened – I sneezed!

Instantly, the light in my parents room flicked on, and my mom and dad came out. I smiled meekly.

"You couldn't sleep either?" I asked, not all that convincingly.

"Nathan!" Dad growled. "Dr. Zabberwatz just called. He said you were in the hospital!"

Mom brought me a towel and dry pj's.

"I...I was just visiting someone," I murmured.

"In the middle of the night?!" he asked angrily. "Especially since I just told you not to go to the hospital!"

"But Dad," I whined, not meaning to, "Mr. Crown looks forward to my visits. And – "

"Mr. Crown! On floor six? Do you have any idea how dangerous it is to be on floor six? Do you?" Dad was losing it, and I was getting very nervous.

"But Dad! I saw sick people with this awful skin disease and...."

Dad's eyes opened wide in horror.

"What did you see?" he asked me, as though what I said hadn't registered.

"This disease...like a burning white brand...disgusting." The words spilled out of me. "Mr. Crown was told he was the only one with it, but I know that isn't true. There must be – "

158

Dad looked like he had just lost his best friend. Or his best son.

"You were in the same room with him?"

"Sure, how else would I know? But don't worry, I kept pretty far away from him (I lied – no sense in getting my parents any more worried). And then – "

My mom started to cry. For a moment, I thought Dad was going to fall over. He held onto the wall to balance himself. My older sister, Tanya, stepped out of her room, rubbing her eyes. She stood next to me.

"What happened?" she asked nervously.

Dad looked at her. Then at me.

"You shouldn't have gone there, Nathan," he told me, putting a heavy hand on my shoulder. "But it's too late now. Come change clothes. We have to go."

Dad looked very sad, and scared. That's when I began to cry.

"Where?" I asked, slowly removing my wet clothes. Mom got me a sweatshirt and boots and found the raincoat I'd been looking for earlier in the day. Dad didn't answer my question. He left for a few moments, then came back, fully dressed.

"To the hospital," Dad said, finally answering my question.

"Why?" I demanded, refusing to budge.

"Because, Nathan, you may have been exposed to a deadly virus. I have to get you into

quarantine."

My father grabbed me tightly by the arm.

"Don't worry Becka, he probably wasn't exposed long enough for anything to happen. I just can't take any chances," Dad said to my mother. "But you'll have to do something for me while I'm gone," he told her.

Mom looked up at him. My wet clothes were in her hands.

"Burn those," Dad ordered, as he walked with me towards the front door.

It seemed to be only occurring in and around Jerusalem, so far. There had been no reports of the disease spreading. For that he was grateful.

His eyes searched and analyzed the clean stones of the houses on Metudela Street. He felt that familiar tingling (more like a scratching really, a scratching inside his body) as he came closer to a house tucked away behind some trees.

Seven green bricks stood out. Green bricks which didn't belong there. During the day it would have been hard to spot the bricks, with so much greenery all around. But he knew what to look for, and where to look. He had been following this particular politician for over two months now.

"When will they learn?" he thought. "Do they think God's patience is forever? Do they think Judgement has left this world?"

He took out a tool box and began to hammer the green stones. The stones crumbled at the hammer's touch.

"Don't kill them," he pleaded under his breath. "Please don't kill them. Remember, You promised that if there were fifty good people, You would let the city live. Is Jerusalem any less than Sodom? Are there not more than fifty good people in this city?"

The noise woke up the residents of the house. The owner of the house came out to see what was happening. He swept his flashlight across the outside of his house, and saw the man holding the hammer.

"Get away from here, right now!" the owner shouted. "Get away! I'm calling the police."

"You don't understand," the man said. "I must rid your house of this plague. And you must repent. You must think of what you have done, before it is too late."

The owner's wife called out to him, "Moshe, what's happening?"

"Call the police!" Moshe called back. But before he could say anything more, the man dragged Moshe off the porch, smothered his face with chloroform, and dragged him, barely breathing, to his waiting car. By now, neighbors were opening their windows to see what was happening, but the man and his quarry were already gone.

"I will make you understand," the man said to the limp body by his side. "I will make you understand before it is too late."

The minute we got into the car, Dad made a call on his cell phone.

"Amnon! My son was just over at the hospital. Floor six. I'm afraid he may have been exposed to Doris."

Exposed to Doris? I wondered. That sounded ridiculous. Didn't Dad know I had visited a man?

"I'm bringing him over now. Have the proper clearance ready for me." My father hung up and turned to me.

"Nathan, we're going to have to run some tests on you to make sure you're okay."

"Just because I spoke with Mr. Crown?" I asked, trying to make my father understand that I didn't even know anyone named Doris.

"Because you breathed the same air he did!" Dad snapped.

"But Dr. Zabberwatz did too," I protested.

"Dr. Zabberwatz has been in contact with these patients from the very first. He's never shown any symptoms in the three months of contact. He seems to have a natural immunity. I'm not sure you do."

"What is it, Dad?"

"It seems to be a new kind of leprosy."

"And if I have it?"

"We'll take it one step at a time. I want to make sure you don't have it, and I need you to cooperate. Okay, Nathan?"

I nodded. Dad had an angry look on his face.

162

"You should never have gone near that patient!"

We parked in front of the hospital. My father helped me out of the car. I think he was afraid I might run away. We marched in, this time through the front doors.

"Hi, Shari! Jeannie!" I smiled hopefully. Jeannie smiled and waved, but Shari started crying. I had never seen a nurse that emotional.

"I guess news travels fast," I laughed. But that only made Dad more anxious.

"What's going to happen now, Dad?" I asked, nervously.

"Nathan, you're just going to have to listen to the doctors. I'm going to try to stay with you for as long as I can."

I stopped abruptly. "What about you, and Mom, and Tanya?"

"The chances that we have it aren't high because it hasn't begun to develop in you, yet."

I wanted to cry again, but I didn't. So much had happened so fast.

We reached the seventh floor. Two guards, with gas masks, were waiting for us.

"I'm Dr. Peters. This is my son, Nathan," Dad announced, putting on a gas mask that one of the guards handed him. I didn't get one.

We were led into what must have been the waiting room at one time. A red-headed man walked up to me, smiling. His smile could not hide the fact

that he was angry.

"Nathan, this is Dr. Rockbe," my father said.

"Okay. We're going to start the decontamination process immediately, just in case. Quarantine may last anywhere between seven to twenty-one days," Dr. Rockbe announced.

Dad nodded and let go of my hand. Rockbe took it.

"Dad?" I didn't want to go with Rockbe. His hand was cold and clammy.

"Okay, Walter," Dr. Rockbe said to my father, in a very cold way. I wondered if he had any kids. If he did, I felt sorry for them. "This is as far as your level of clearance permits you to go. I'll take it from here."

"Come on, Amnon," my father pleaded, "I'm part of the team. He's my son. Do this one favor for me. Let me in, just this once."

For a moment, I thought Dr. Rockbe would agree. But then that cold look covered his face.

"Walter, you know it's more complicated than that. It's not that I don't want to do you a favor. I can't. I'm sorry, Walter. But we will keep you informed."

I could sense my father's deep disappointment. My father smiled at me, and told me not to worry. Then he leaned over to Dr. Rockbe.

"He's my son! I want to be kept informed of everything that goes on with him. I'll hold you responsible if there are any mistakes or errors in his treatment. Remember that.

"And Amnon," my father said, his voice

sounding like death itself, "if he disappears like some of the others, you *will* pay for it."

I had never heard Dad talk like that. It gave me the chills. Dr. Rockbe started to open his mouth as though to protest, but then changed his mind. He turned and led me into a room with tons of weird-looking suits. He put one on.

"This is called a Bio-Hazard suit, Nathan. This is a special suit which no known organism can penetrate. I'm going to have to put this helmet on me so it will work. I will hand signal you from here on."

"Don't I get one?" I asked.

"At this point, if you're not infected, the sterile atmosphere we're about to enter won't harm you. If you are infected, the atmosphere might help you to fight against the disease. I'm going to conduct some experiments that could be dangerous for me without this suit. That's why I'm wearing one."

As he put the helmet over his head, I shouted, "Wait! I just thought I should tell you, I never even met Doris!" I confessed.

"I hope that's true," Dr. Rockbe said, looking sad.

"Wouldn't I know if I met her?" I asked.

"Not necessarily," he answered. "You see, Doris isn't a person. It's the name of the disease we're fighting. Doris was the first person who had the disease," he said, as he lifted the helmet over his head. "And the first to disappear," he whispered, as

he secured the helmet onto his head.

Disappear?

But before I could ask another question, Dr. Rockbe was on the move. He looked sort of creepy. He walked very slowly, like he was moving through water. Then he pushed me through a door.

First, we went into some tunnel where different colored smoke swirled around me, creating really cool patterns. Then, just as I was getting used to the colors, a blast of wind from a huge fan slammed into my face and I fell to the ground. Dr. Rockbe must have been expecting the wind because he held onto something just before I got blasted. After a moment, he lifted me by my arm and brought me into another room. This one was full of all sorts of machinery. There was a clear plastic bubble in the middle of the room, and a bed and desk inside the bubble. There were tons of weird-looking hoses attached to the bubble from the inside and the outside.

Dr. Rockbe patted my head, and then he was gone.

"Who-who are you?" Moshe asked.

"I am the Kohen Gadol," said his captor. "As the Torah says, The Kohen shall look at the affliction, and if indeed the affliction is in the walls of the house, then your house is afflicted with tzara'at.

"You have been warned by God!"

"What are you talking about?" Moshe asked, beginning to get angry. "Isn't tzara'at some sort of

leprosy that they talk about in the Bible? There's no such thing anymore. Wake up, there's no leprosy in Jerusalem – not anywhere in Israel. Take me home!" he commanded.

"You don't understand. We must remove the stones. We must cast away the contamination."

"Will you stop talking like that!" demanded Moshe. "What stones? What are you talking about? Listen, I'm an important man. People will come looking for me. You must let me go. I promise I will forget about this entire incident. But you must let me go. Now!"

The Kohen moved closer to the man. As if to ward him away, the man lifted his hand in front of his face. The Kohen looked at the hand and drew back, hastily.

"Aiee!" he shouted. "It is too late. Too late! Look!" He pointed to a bright white spot on the man's forearm. "It has begun."

"What are you talking about?" asked the man, looking at his forearm. "I've had that white spot for over a week. Some sort of skin discoloration. What has that to do with leprosy?"

The Kohen didn't answer right away. He took the man's arm, examining the spot, and intoned –

The Kohen shall set the person aside for a second seven-day period.

With that, he got up and left the man.

Moshe heard the door lock.

"Seven days?" he wondered. A shiver traveled down his spine.

I was sitting inside a plastic bubble, thinking about the weird man who had just run in, looked me over, and run out again. He didn't have a suit on.

I'm not really sure it happened, though. I find that I doze off all the time. I have no way of telling the difference between day and night, and time gets a bit fuzzy for me.

I had tons of tests run on me, all by people in those funny suits. Sometimes they spoke to me, other times they were too busy for that. There were always a bunch of doctors hanging around, staring at me. They would stare at me for hours at a time, like I was a TV or something. Normally, I would stare back.

Once, this really serious doctor was staring at me with wide eyes. So I did a cartwheel. That didn't impress her. Then I made faces. She blinked, and left.

Now, the doctors weren't even staring at me. They were reading charts. I was bored and sort of depressed. I didn't know what would happen to me, but no matter what, I wanted to find out why people were disappearing. I had overheard one doctor say that four people had disappeared from their rooms within the last three months. How could they disappear inside a hospital – inside a room like this?

The days crept by. I didn't hear from my parents, but I knew they must be worried. I did

overhear one of the doctors say that the seventh and eighth floors were filling up with patients. They all seemed to have a new kind of leprosy. The truth is, I didn't understand what they were saying. What's leprosy?

Then, just as I was thinking of making a break for it, the lights suddenly went out. The doctors outside my bubble were very upset and went to get help. I forced myself to get up, thinking that this might be my chance to run away. I had had it. I realized, even if they didn't, that there was nothing wrong with me that twelve hours of sleep wouldn't cure.

I slowly made my way to the plastic door. As I reached it, someone reached in and pulled me out. Before I could say anything, a strange smell made me feel even more tired than I was.

"Oh well," I said to myself, "maybe now I can get some sleep."

When I woke up, I found myself in another room. A regular room. I could hear what sounded like rain outside. The room was dark, so I searched the walls for a light switch. I found it and flicked it up. There was a table inside the room, and there was food and water on the table. I drank some water.

"Who are you?" someone asked me.

I looked around and then noticed, for the first time, that there was a cot at the far end of the room. Someone was sleeping on it.

"I'm Nathan," I answered. "Who are you?"

"I'm Moshe. Moshe Veiss," the man answered. "Did he capture you, too?"

"I don't know," I honestly answered. "Am I captured? I've been in a hospital ward inside a small plastic bubble for so long, this seems like freedom to me. What are you doing here?"

"There's this crazy guy. He thinks he's a Kohen Gadol, some sort of high priest or something. He says he has to lock me away for seven days. Says I have tzara'at."

"Is that the leprosy everyone's been talking about?" I asked.

"It's nothing. Just a white spot on my arm. There is no such thing as leprosy in Israel," he insisted. "This guy is just crazy. We have to figure out how to get out of here."

"Isn't tzara'at a disease in the Torah?" I asked him, recalling my studies in school. Now I began to remember that leprosy was a skin disease. But tzara'at was a disease that affected the skin, clothes, even houses. I had read about it when we studied the third book of the Torah, Leviticus, in school. The teacher sort of quickly went over it. No one really understood what was going on, except that you got tzara'at, or at least the Israelites did, for one basic reason – speaking evil about someone.

"This crazy guy thinks I've got it," Moshe explained. "He says I have to be 'set aside,' or something like that, for seven days. What's going on?"

"That's what it says in the Torah," I explained.

"The Kohen looks at the disease and decides whether to set the person aside for seven days – I think they call it quarantine – and after the seven days, if the Kohen decides the disease is getting better, then the man is cured."

"And if not?" Moshe asked.

"Then the man is contaminated and has to stay away from everyone until he becomes cured."

"How is that supposed to happen?" Moshe wanted to know.

"I'm not sure," I said. "I think you're supposed to think about the bad things you said and then, if you're really sorry, the tzara'at goes away. I think."

"What has that got to do with my house?" he asked.

"That's easy," I told him. "Houses and clothes of the person get tzara'at first. It's a kind of warning to the person that he is doing something wrong. If he doesn't listen then – POW! – he gets tzara'at on his body."

"Come here," he ordered.

Slowly, I walked over to him. When I was very close, he held up his hand. I bent down to shake it, but that's not what he wanted.

"Look at this white spot. Is it tzara'at?"

I looked. It looked like a white spot. A little like what Mr. Crown had. I didn't think it was dangerous, though, but what did I know?

"I have no idea," I admitted. "I'm only in seventh grade. And I'm not even a Kohen. Has it spread?"

"Yes," Moshe said, as though he were pronouncing a death sentence on himself.

"Well, don't worry. I never heard of anyone ever dying of tzara'at," I said, trying to make him feel better. The truth is, I never heard of anyone ever having tzara'at! And I didn't remember whether you died from it or not.

Just then, the Kohen came in.

"Are you ready?" he asked me, ignoring Moshe.

"Ready for what?" I countered, beginning to get scared.

"Let me see your hands," the Kohen ordered. I held them out. "Now your head," he said, dropping my hands and peering intently at my scalp. "Any loss of hair recently?" he asked in a doctor-like manner.

"No," I answered, "although I do have a little dandruff."

The Kohen continued to search my head. Finally, he folded his hands and, looking me straight in the eye, announced, "You're pure."

"Pure?"

"Pure," he repeated.

"As in 100% pure orange juice?" I joked.

The Kohen chose to ignore my humor. "Why did they keep you isolated so long?"

"I think they thought I had caught something from the guy I was visiting in the hospital."

"Don't they know by now that tzara'at is a disease borne by the tongue, not by the air?" he

mumbled to himself. "What fools! What utter fools!"

The Kohen stomped out of the room, leaving me and Moshe alone.

"Well, at least *you're* not contaminated," Moshe said, with just a hint of jealously. "At least *you* won't die."

I was getting pretty uncomfortable with all this dying stuff. And, as far as being *pure* was concerned, truthfully, I had no idea what the Kohen meant.

Why would I get tzara'at? Sure, I speak a few words of gossip now and then, but hey, who doesn't? And sure, I occasionally say things I shouldn't, but what kid doesn't?

"What do you do?" I asked Moshe.

"I work for the government."

"Excuse me for asking," I said, feeling slightly uncomfortable, "but do you like, speak evil a lot?"

Moshe looked at me as though I had just asked him if he drank blood.

"Don't tell me you believe in this tzara'at garbage. Everyone speaks a few words of evil now and then. You don't see everyone running around with leprosy, do you?"

"Maybe it's a question of how much," I suggested. "Maybe only those who speak evil a lot, or say things that put other people down, or talk about others when they shouldn't...maybe if they keep doing this for a long time...maybe then they get tzara'at."

"But why now?" Moshe asked. "People have

been talking evil for thousands of years *after* the Jews came out of the desert. You've never heard of anyone getting tzara'at in all those years, have you?"

Moshe had a point. I had wondered the same thing myself.

"I think this Kohen is crazy," Moshe repeated for about the hundredth time. "He's one of those fanatics you find in Jerusalem. One of those people who thinks he knows the ways of God and sees the end of the world over the horizon."

"Well, you have to admit that there is something strange about this disease. All the people in the hospital kept getting worse and worse. No medicines seemed to work. I don't know..." I let my voice trail off.

"But I sure do know that I have to get out of here," I concluded. "I don't know where we are, but I've got the feeling we're still in Jerusalem. Let's – "

Just then, the Kohen walked in. Moshe and I must have looked very guilty because he said, accusingly, "What are you two up to? Do you think you can leave before you are cured? Would a Kohen allow one smitten with tzara'at to leave confinement before his time? Never!"

"But sir," Moshe began, deciding to take the logical approach, "I don't feel sick. Not really. Just tired. But who wouldn't be, locked up in here, eating only bread and water. Why don't you let us leave? If you want to save the world, that's your business. We just want to leave."

The Kohen moved closer to Moshe and lifted

his hand. The white spot on Moshe's hand seemed to be growing and getting deeper into his skin, even as we looked at it.

"I have no pain!" Moshe exclaimed, pulling his hand out of the Kohen's grip.

"Not yet," the Kohen said. "But soon you will feel what others have felt, and then it will be too late. Too late for forgiveness. Not because God would not accept your forgiveness, but because you have forgotten how to ask for it."

"Er, Mr. Kohen," I said, hesitantly, "I have spoken evil too. Who hasn't? And I don't have any spots, or whatever it is you are looking for."

The Kohen thought about that for a moment.

"You are not twenty yet," he answered. "And you freely admit your sins. That is an important step, a step everyone must take before being declared 'pure.'"

"What does being twenty have to do with it?" I asked.

"Our rabbis have said, 'Until a person is twenty, the heavenly court reserves judgment on his sins. Once he has reached twenty, judgment is rendered.'"

"So why am I here?" I wondered out loud.

"You have a purpose here, Nachum son of Isaiah the Levi," he intoned as though calling me up to the Torah. "And you will soon know it."

Moshe rolled his eyes at me, signaling that the

Kohen was crazy. I just shrugged.

The Kohen looked at me, and for a moment, I felt...like...like he was trying to tell me something with his eyes. But then Moshe shouted, "Get us out of here you crazy fool!" and the spell was broken.

The Kohen left again, and I began my search to find a way out.

"Why don't we just attack him?" I asked Moshe.

"I tried that soon after I got here. He's very strong. He pushed me away like I was a baby. That's how I sprained my ankle."

I hadn't noticed before, but his left ankle was bandaged.

"Maybe, if you distract him, I might be able to come up from behind and hit him with something," Moshe suggested. "Only – if it doesn't work, I'm afraid he'll kill us."

I shrugged again, and began searching the room for ways out. There was a small window, but it had the standard Israeli metal bars on it. The door was locked from the outside. There was another door, but it was locked too. There were probably more "victims" of the Kohen being quarantined on the other side.

I gave up.

Moshe and I were busy talking about how we could attract attention from those outside the building, when I heard what sounded like a very strong explosion. The room shook. The pitcher on the table jumped up, landed back on the table,

tottered, and then flipped on its side, finally rolling off with a loud "crash!"

Two seconds later, we heard voices on the other side of the front door.

"Stand back," a voice warned. "Stand back! We're going to blow it!"

"Kapow!" the door blew inward, just as Moshe and I hit the ground. Moshe yelled, "Ow!" and I was sure he had been hit by some shrapnel from the door. But it was only his leg. He had fallen on his bad ankle.

Three men burst into the room. They were dressed in space suits, not unlike the ones worn in the hospital. But these guys weren't doctors; they were some sort of police unit. I couldn't help but notice that they didn't carry guns. Then I realized that with their protective gloves, they wouldn't have been able to pull the trigger of a gun, anyway.

They couldn't talk either, except to each other. They motioned for us to follow them, but they wouldn't come near either of us. I helped Moshe get up, and he hopped after them as fast as he could. I followed.

We went through a corridor and then into the kitchen. There was plenty of smoke everywhere. The three guys motioned for us to hurry. They headed out of the kitchen and into a living room where the Kohen waited.

He stood there, wearing a white robe and a strange looking hat. Even though there was thick, strange-smelling smoke in the living room, I

remembered seeing a picture of that hat in a book my father bought me for my Bar Mitzvah. It was the hat of the Kohen Gadol, the High Priest in the Temple.

"And the person with tzara'at...," the Kohen shouted, pointing at Moshe, *"his garments shall be ripped, his hair shall be cut off, and he shall clothe himself from foot to head, covering his mouth with his cloak."*

Moshe and I stood frozen. The Kohen was such a strange sight, especially in the smoke-filled room. He almost looked like a ghost.

"The contaminated one is to call out so that all will hear – 'Contaminated! I am contaminated!'"

The three policemen-soldiers weren't interested in the Kohen's speech. But they were interested in the fact that he was standing between them and the front door.

So, they charged.

The Kohen stood his ground. He took the full force of their attack, head on. But instead of falling over – as any normal person would have – the Kohen pushed the three of them into the air. I know. It sounds impossible. But that's what he did. They flew back like three bowling balls in search of a lane.

"Contaminated!" the Kohen shouted again.

Two of the three men were either too stunned or too afraid to get up. The third sat up, but seemed in no hurry to face the Kohen again. He was talking inside his suit.

"All the days that the affliction is upon him he shall remain contaminated," the Kohen continued,

stepping over one of the seemingly lifeless policemen, straight towards me.

"He is contaminated! He shall live in isolation. He shall live outside the camp of Israel!"

The Kohen grabbed me. Before I could say a thing, he lifted me in his arms and ran outside. I saw, out of the corner of my eye, a line of police cars headed our way.

That's when I started to fight back. I thought that if I could just hold him off for a few moments, maybe make him fall, that would give me enough time to escape, or at least give the police a chance to rescue me.

But I should have known better.

The Kohen reached his car in three giant leaps. He shoved me into the back seat, locked the door, raced around the front, got in, and off we went, with the police cars not far behind. All this time, I couldn't help wondering if Moshe was okay. He had thought that the Kohen was coming for him and fell to the ground, pleading not to be hurt. But the Kohen had just mumbled *"Contaminated!"* again, and then grabbed me.

I was watching the police cars behind us racing up Aza Street, trying hard to follow as we turned onto King George Street. I suppose I should have done something to distract the Kohen, but while I was scared to death, it was also very exciting.

I realized that, instead of finding the person who was snatching people from the hospital, the

snatcher had found me. I also realized that I wasn't much of a detective. But I really didn't care. What mattered now was how the Kohen would lose all those police cars.

Yeah, I found myself cheering for him.

Don't ask me why.

Anyway, we zoomed down King George, made a right down Hillel Street, flew around cars coming at us from just about everywhere, and turned right at the parking lot – a one way (not our way) street – and shot out into Agron Street. Right again, back to Aza Street, and well...around and around until we parked in an underground parking space somewhere on Rashbah Street.

I was dizzy. So, it seemed, were the police. They were going every which way, up and down one-way streets, sometimes driving into each other, but they didn't find us. The underground parking space was too well hidden.

It was only when the Kohen turned to me and said, "Now, Nachum son of Isaiah the Levi, we will talk," that I really began to worry.

It's been almost a year now since I joined the Kohen, whose real name is Aaron Lev HaKohen. I'm allowed one phone call a week to my parents, just so they know I'm alive and kicking.

Of course, they're still looking for me.

In the beginning, I used to leave signs like

candy wrappers with my name scribbled on the inside, and even pieces of clothing, near the houses that we checked. But since we never stayed in the same place for more than a week, there was no way my parents could find me.

Escape?

I tried that too. At first, the Kohen actually tied me up to him, giving me just enough leeway to walk a few feet from him. Eventually, he didn't tie me up anymore. So I tried to run away, but he was fast – real fast.

Finally, I decided to wait until I thought the Kohen was sleeping. Go figure – the man doesn't sleep. I mean it. He doesn't sleep. At least not that I have ever seen.

We usually search for tzara'at houses about three days a week. Mostly at night, but sometimes during the late afternoon. I know the routine pretty well by now. We case a house that looks like the stones are discolored, and then we go there when the owners are away. If the place is contaminated, well, then we wait for the owner and grab him.

Don't ask. I usually just keep the car running. At least I'm getting free driving lessons out of all this.

Once we quarantine the owner of the house, Aaron tries to convince him to repent, or at least recognize that he is speaking evil.

Sometimes, it works.

Usually, it doesn't.

If we're too late, and the tzara'at has started spreading, I call the police or the hospital, and they come and pick the fellow up. No one has figured out that all those cases of "leprosy," as the doctors continue to call it, are being called in by a kid. Me.

My parents want me to come home. I've talked it over with Aaron. He says I have God's work to do. What with the Messiah coming and everything, he doesn't want me to waste time when there is so much to do. He says – and I sort of believe him – that the only thing holding up the Messiah is all the people speaking evil. That's why God brought back tzara'at. To get people back on track.

Considering the number of people we've quarantined lately – and the number that Aaron has convinced to stop talking evil – I'd say that God's plan is working.

Aaron believes he's been chosen to be the Kohen Gadol when the Messiah comes and the Temple is built.

He wants me to be a leader among the Levites. So, he's been teaching me about the duties of the Levites.

A singer, I'm not.

But I've got good strong shoulders, and when the time comes – so Aaron says – I'll be chosen to carry the Holy Ark.

We're talking years, of course. But at least The End (Beginning?) is in sight.

Until then, I help Aaron as much as I can. Although, to be honest, I do get homesick once in a

while. Actually, I've been planning to visit my parents. Now that Aaron doesn't watch me so closely (I even go to the makolet – the local grocery store – for him), I figured I'd sneak away for a couple of hours and visit my folks and my sister.

I was going to go this evening. Right after we checked out a house Aaron has been watching for over a week.

When we got there, it was very dark. I held the flashlight – these days, Aaron's trusting me with more than the getaway car – while Aaron checked the stones. They were very green.

So we waited until the owner came home.

Boy, was Dad ever surprised to see me.